Universal Chronicles
Extermination
2991

Universal Chronicles
Extermination
2991

Written by
Dan Lee

One Garden
Publishing

For my foster brothers and sisters:

Miles and Aubrey

For my foster brothers and sister, that passed away:

Travis, Mark, Tracy

To my foster dad who passed away:

Bernie

To my foster mom:

Moreen

PROLOGUE

Many years ago, humanity embarked on a bold journey, one that spanned the stars and saw the birth of a new era. Multiple distant planets and solar systems, each teeming with their own challenges and wonders, became the new home for Earth's wayward children. As they ventured deeper into the unknown, humanity discovered they were not alone. Across the cosmic expanse, diverse alien civilizations awaited, some hostile, others curious, and a rare few open to friendship.

This expansion, however, was anything but smooth. The early years were marked by famine, deadly plagues that ravaged colonies, and relentless conflicts against enigmatic extraterrestrial foes. Dark forces seemed to emerge from every corner of the galaxy, threatening to extinguish the flickering light of human ambition. It was through intricate negotiations, fragile alliances, and sheer determination that the Universal Peacekeeping Federation (UPF) was born—a beacon of hope in the tumultuous cosmos.

In the year 2991, this federation, consisting of both humans and alien species, has become the steadfast guardian of peace. A council has been established to govern the complex laws that now bind hundreds of civilizations together, from the towering Zor'khan warriors to the highly intelligent Calidorfians. At the heart of this vast organization is the central headquarters, a place where galaxy-wide operations are coordinated, ensuring the delicate balance between war and peace is maintained.

The UPF military forces are organized into regional headquarters, each managing the UPF's presence in various sectors of the galaxy. These headquarters are responsible for safeguarding their assigned regions and overseeing the day-to-day operations of their bases. Each base is supported by specialized teams focused on discovery, defense, or reconnaissance. Officers are divided into three distinct classes, each equipped with advanced ULTRA suits designed to enhance their abilities in the field. Whether commanding battles, healing the wounded, or defending ships from attack, these specialized suits are essential to their survival.

But not all welcome this new unity. Separatist factions, both human and alien, see the UPF as a threat to their autonomy and power. These rebels cling to their influence, waging shadow wars across the galaxy, sowing discord and chaos. Yet, amidst the conflict, whispers of something far more terrifying begins to circulate—an enemy with motives unknown, a force shrouded in secrecy, that threatens to upend the fragile peace. As the galaxy teeters on a precarious balance, this force stirs once more.

CHAPTER ONE

Evander Guryon stands staring out a window, reminiscing about the tragic loss of his mother, Tessa Guryon. To this day, the events of the accident that took her life, still haunts him. He was there the day she died, just a young boy, and the events left him traumatized. He remembers how both her and his dad would read to him a bedtime story from his favourite book series, "Tale of Two Worlds", a story based around acceptance and understanding no matter what a person might look or sound like. Both his mother and father worked for an organization called Universal Peacekeeping Federation, or UPF for short. They worked side by side in their shared laboratory at the UPF central headquarters, on the planet, Arigold. He can still remember the shock and horror on his dad's face when he found out about the death of his wife. To this day, Doctor Guryon works tirelessly, developing new and better armour. His crowning achievement is the ULTRA suit, which stands for Ultimate Lightweight Tactical Reinforced Armour, utilizing bleeding edge technology. He made multiple variants depending on the situation that a person might be in. Doctor Guryon works so much, that he doesn't get a chance to spend time with his son, something Evander wishes he would. However, this doesn't stop him from trying to spend time with him, even to the point of joining the UPF himself.

As he is reminiscing, he doesn't hear or notice someone hurling an object at him. "Catch, dumbass!" a five-armed officer jeered, hurling a can of juice directly at Evander's head.

Rubbing his sore spot, he responds with a touch of sarcasm, "Oh, how thoughtful of you!" Evander glances at the small translator device each of them wore, double-checking that it isn't damaged. It is simple tech really, but it bridges the gap between countless tongues and dialects.

Evander turns around to look at the person. As he is doing so, he sees another officer approach, wearing a curious expression. It is his long-time friend, Angelica Tenah. She is tall, with an athletic build, her hair tied back in the style of a bun. As she is approaching, she is adjusting her uniform, which is always clean and well put together. "Why do you allow them to treat you like that, Evan?" she questions.

Meeting her gaze, Evan flashes a smile and replies, "Why waste my breath on someone who clearly isn't interested in a meaningful conversation?" He takes a moment to gather himself before continuing, "Besides, I could use a drink anyway. Thanks for your concern, Ange." With a swift motion, Evander retrieves the can and cracks it open, taking a refreshing sip.

As Angelica and Evander make their way toward the meeting center, for their orientation session and to meet their new commander, Angelica sports a sly smile, her words laced with gentle reproach. "You're truly incorrigible, Evan. Always letting others trample over you, subjecting you to ridicule."

Evander lets out a weary sigh, his gaze fixed on the path ahead. "I choose not to engage in retaliation," he explains. Pausing momentarily, he turns to face Angelica, his expression earnest. "What purpose does it serve when it often leads to unnecessary conflict and potentially spiraling into physical violence? You know how much I dislike such confrontations."

Upon reaching the meeting room, Angelica turns toward Evander, her eyes carrying a hint of conviction. "You can't deny that there are moments when violence becomes a necessary means to an end. It all depends on the situation."

In response, Evander smirks and replies, "Guess I'll have to count on avoiding such situations then." With that, they proceed together into the meeting room, joining a group of new graduates already gathered.

The commander's piercing gaze falls upon Evander and Angelica, directing them to two seats. As Evander settles into his chair, his voice thunders, "MY NAME IS DRIXEN! BUT YOU WILL ADDRESS ME AS COMMANDER DRIXEN!" His attention now fixes on Evander, he bellows, "WHAT'S YOUR NAME, OFFICER? NAME AND CLASSIFICATION! NOW!"

Evander feels a tremor of unease, but manages to compose himself and responds, "Evander Guryon, sir! Of the STAR class sir!"

Drixen takes a deep breath, his voice resonating with authority. "LOUDER ENSIGN! WHAT IS YOUR NAME AND CLASSIFICATION?"

Inhaling deeply, Evander musters his courage and shouts, "EVANDER GURYON, SIR! OF THE STAR CLASS, SIR!"

The commander leans forward, his voice stern and resolute. "IF YOU BELIEVE YOU'RE FIT FOR THE STAR CLASSIFICATION, THEN YOU BEST LEARN TO RAISE YOUR VOICE!"

Evander's face flushes and is relieved when Commander Drixen's attention shifts away from him. The STAR class is considered the elite classification of the UPF. The officers specialize in tactical planning and leadership. Evander hates the constant elevated expectations put upon him because of his chosen career path—the only solace is that he has the constant support of Angelica, who is also in the STAR class.

Drixen turns his attention to Angelica, who remains composed, her gaze fixed straight ahead at the wall monitor. "WHAT IS YOUR NAME AND CLASSIFICATION?"

Angelica promptly responds, her voice carrying determination. "ANGELICA TENAH, SIR! MY CLASSIFICATION IS STAR!"

A flicker of satisfaction dances across Drixen's face. "That's the spirit!" he remarks, pleased with Angelica's assertiveness. Angelica is not phased. Unlike Evan, who just graduated with his class and has been given the rank of ensign, Angelica completed her training a year ago. She breezed through her academy classes and exercises while maintaining top scores, despite the extra workload, earning her early graduation. Since then, she has been on multiple assignments and has been recently given the rank of lieutenant. After waiting a year, her class has caught up to her and she finally gets to re-join them in their first mission.

While Commander Drixen continues addressing the group, two latecomers, Blarek and Kal'korg, enter the room, looking around cautiously and spotting their friends, Evander and Angelica. Blarek is a tall, stocky person from the planet Pheo, and has a serious, but friendly, demeanor. He has a feline look to him with hazel eyes, dark-grey skin and black-blue hair, brushed back neatly over his cat-like ears. Kal'korg is medium sized and slender, with a friendly smile, a large nose and ears that remind his human friends of a Koala, and a disheveled mane of hair that seems to magically avoid falling into his eyes. He's from the planet Ho'gren, an easy-going race, with short, pale-green fur, which seems to change hue depending on their emotions.

The commander arches his left eyebrow in mild annoyance. "You two," he exclaims, "are LATE!" He gestures toward a pair of chairs situated behind Evander and Angelica. His frustration apparent, he demands, "WHAT ARE YOUR NAMES, CLASSIFICATIONS, AND REASON FOR YOUR TARDINESS?"

The two ensigns, visibly flustered, freeze where they stand. Blarek responds first, "Ensign Blarek Ta'yash of the METEOR class, sir…" Blarek gets cut off as he is about to explain his reason.

Commander Drixen's voice raises, "SPEAK UP ENSIGN! WHAT IS YOUR NAME AND CLASSIFICATION AND YOUR REASON?"

Steadying himself, Blarek responds loudly, "ENSIGN BLAREK TA'YASH OF THE METEOR CLASS, SIR! WE DON'T HAVE A GOOD EXCUSE SIR! WE'RE LATE BECAUSE WE SLEPT IN!"

Commander Drixen scowls. Blarek stands focusing straight ahead, trying to ignore the commander's stare. The METEOR class is for officers focused on security, piloting, and other tactical activities. They are prepared for the front lines, whether they're securing outposts or piloting starships through enemy fire. Blarek is rarely worried about himself, but he is often worried about his gentle and fun-loving companion, Kal'korg, who is standing nervously next to him, his gaze darting around.

Commander Drixen's attention moves to Kal'korg, whose voice tinged with embarrassment, responds, "Ensign Kal'korg Zarao of the MOON class, sir."

The commander is directly in front of Kal'korg, and his voice booms in response, "DID YOU NOT HEAR WHAT I TOLD YOUR COMRADE? SPEAK LOUDER! NO ONE IN THE BACK HEARD THAT!"

Kal'korg flinches in response, the loud voice of Commander Drixen merely inches away. MOON-class officers are the scientists, engineers, and medics of the UPF. Kal'korg has trained as a medical officer, staying away from the perils of battle. His experience is in healing the sick or wounded, performing medical procedures, or sometimes doing data analysis for research purposes. He lacks Blarek's stoic demeanor when facing an adversary.

Kal'korg, summoning his courage, takes a deep breath and raises his voice. "ENSIGN KAL'KORG ZARAO OF THE MOON CLASS, SIR!"

Drixen, satisfied with the volume of the response, returns to the view board. "NOW SIT DOWN, AND YOU BETTER PAY ATTENTION!" he commands, his words carrying a stern warning.

The Commander delves into an explanation of the ensigns' uniforms, captivating their attention. "There are three distinct types of suits, each possessing its own unique qualities," he emphasizes, gesturing toward the viewing board. The display illuminates, showcasing the first suit. "This is the ULTRA suit," he continues, "equipped with universal transponders and a trans-universal encrypted interlink, as most of you are already aware. They all have advanced shielding, making it difficult for most firearms to penetrate."

The image shifts, revealing the Z10 version of the suit. "The Z10 variation is predominantly utilized by the STAR classes. It offers enhanced stealth capabilities for reconnaissance missions and an upgraded heads-up display, or HUD, that enables users to magnify their surroundings while benefiting from infrared and heat signature detection."

The viewing board transitions to focus solely on the suit's body. "Observe the Z10's micro motors and air converter," the commander points out, "enabling you to breathe in space without relying on additional cumbersome equipment. Its advanced poly-weave fibers are reinforced with carbon nanotubes, which offer exceptional flexibility and protection, while the gold-accented shoulder plates contain built-in sensory enhancers for improved situational awareness."

Evan sits forward in his seat, listening intently. The ULTRA STAR suit's advanced communication systems and cognitive processors help them strategize in real-time, manage battlefield scenarios, and command missions with precision. They also offer superior mobility and defense, ensuring the leaders in the STAR class can guide their teams through the most dangerous situations. Wearing the suit and learning how to master its features has been Evander's favorite part of his training, and he is eager to learn about the features of the latest model.

Commander Drixen continues, "The Z10 also features a kinetic energy redistribution system, which can absorb and redirect small impacts, making it ideal for stealth operations in hazardous environments. Unlike its predecessor, the Z09, which lacked this feature, the Z10 is designed for both reconnaissance and close combat."

He steps aside, allowing the officers to fully observe the sleek design of the Z10 suit as it rotates on the display. "This is the pinnacle of our STAR Class gear—agile, nearly invisible in the field, and equipped with everything you need to outmaneuver any enemy"

The commander moves on to the next suit, the display revealing a new model with striking orange highlights that trace the sleek contours of its black exterior. "This is the Y10 version, primarily utilized by the METEOR Classes," he explains, his voice steady and authoritative. "While visually similar to the other models, its functionality is tailored to the intense demands of physical labor, security, and heavy-duty piloting." He gestures toward the display, which zooms in on the armor's key components.

Blarek's cat-like ears perk up as he takes in the details of the latest features of his class's suit. After a short pause, Commander Drixen continues with his explanation. "The Y10's reinforced exoskeleton is integrated with enhanced motor servos, allowing the wearer to lift and carry heavy equipment or materials with minimal effort. Its kinetic dampeners are designed to absorb shock from both impacts and high-velocity movements, making it ideal for combat and heavy construction tasks alike. Additionally, the suit's external plating is coated with a heat-resistant material, allowing the wearer to operate in extreme temperatures, such as those found near reactors or volatile environments."

He then points to the orange highlights. "These micro-thrusters embedded in the shoulders provide brief bursts of controlled propulsion, allowing for movement in zero gravity or rapid maneuvers in atmosphere. The suit also includes a basic flight assist system, perfect for navigating complex terrain or low-gravity environments without additional equipment."

The Commander pauses again, allowing the officers to absorb the gravity of the suit's capabilities. "The Y10 is not just a suit, it's a tool for survival in the most hostile of conditions. Whether you're on a starship or an unstable planet's surface, it will protect you and enhance your natural abilities."

The viewing board shifted once again, this time highlighting the X9 version, marked by its deep red highlights that follow the same sharp lines and functional design as the Y10. "Now, we turn our attention to the X9 suit, predominantly used by the MOON Classes," the Commander announces, his tone shifting to one of admiration. "This suit, though similar in appearance to the Y10, has a focus on medical and scientific operations."

Commander Drixen gestures as the viewing board highlights the X9's key systems. This time, it is Kal'korg who's sitting with raptured attention, a grin forming on his face. The commander continues, "The X9 is equipped with advanced medical diagnostics, allowing the wearer to perform emergency medical scans and triage in the field. Its built-in analyzers can detect everything from chemical contaminants to biological pathogens in real-time. Additionally, the suit's red highlights serve more than just an aesthetic purpose—they function as bio-indicators, glowing brighter in response to fluctuations in the wearer's vitals or environmental threats, providing immediate feedback to both the user and their team."

The display zooms in on the suit's chest plate, showing intricate sensor arrays. "The X9's enhanced sensor arrays are designed to analyze molecular structures, making it indispensable for scientific research and medical emergency response. Whether scanning a foreign atmosphere or determining the cause of illness, this suit puts advanced diagnostic power directly at your fingertips."

With a final gesture, the commander allows the officers a moment to appreciate the craftsmanship, then continues, "In sum, the X9 suit is a field medic's lifeline, offering all the protective capabilities of the ULTRA series while providing unparalleled access to life-saving technology."

CHAPTER TWO

At the end of the briefing, Commander Drixen dismisses the group of junior officers for the day, and Evander and Angelica head outside to enjoy the beautiful weather together. The UPF central headquarters is sprawled across a vast campus, its buildings interconnected by winding pathways illuminated by a procession of lights. Lush greenspaces punctuated by meticulously manicured gardens and shrubs adorned the surroundings, lending an air of serenity to the technologically advanced hub of interstellar operations. A while later, Evander and Angelica opt for some training and make their way to the training center. They head toward the entrance of the sparring area, which is located on the furthest side of the building from the meeting center. Along the path, they unexpectedly run into their two friends. "Hey Kal'korg and Blarek, what are you two up to? Care to join us for some sparring?"

Evander grins nervously at Angelica's suggestion, remarking, "More like another beatdown awaits me."

Angelica smiles in response, teasingly adding, "Well, if you dedicated more time to practice, perhaps you'd stand a chance against me once in a while!"

Kal'korg runs his hand down his face, exasperated. "I would have loved to join you, but Blarek here lost his temper," he explains in a hushed tone. "You know how Pheonians can be — thick-headed and fiercely protective."

Blarek shoots Kal'korg a piercing glare, the tension between them palpable.

Kal'korg lets out a sigh, resigned to the consequences. "Thanks to him," he mutters, "we both have to scrub the washrooms for a week and do two hours of base running each day." Blarek simply nods, acknowledging his part in the disciplinary action.

Angelica's curiosity remains unsatisfied. "Firstly, what exactly happened?" she inquires, her gaze fixes on Blarek. "And secondly, why are both of you being punished? Shouldn't it just be Blarek?"

Kal'korg looks at Blarek and explains the situation. "Because this numbskull here exploded in anger and threw the person into our room without even opening the door first," he recounts. "And then, in the midst of the chaos, I accidentally tossed him right onto the lieutenant who came to investigate the commotion."

Blarek nods once again, unable to speak. Evander grows puzzled and asks, "Why isn't Blarek speaking?"

Kal'korg glances at Blarek and then back at Evander. "His mouth got glued shut. We were actually on our way to the infirmary to get the glue removed."

Angelica, perplexed by the situation asks, "Wait, why was his mouth glued in the first place?"

Kal'korg replies nonchalantly, "Oh, you know, the usual. Blarek ran his mouth off to the wrong person."

Angelica sighs, already familiar with who this 'wrong person' can be. "Let me guess... Jalerg!" she exclaims. "Why hasn't he been court-martialed already?" she questions, shaking her head in disbelief.

"Beats us," Kal'korg responds with a chuckle, "but we better head to the infirmary and get his mouth unstuck. It's getting close to lunchtime, and we all know how much Blarek loves pigging out then."

Blarek glares and mutters something incoherent.

"Oh, don't deny it, you know it's true," Kal'korg teases, prompting only a shrug and nod from Blarek. "Catch you guys later." Kal'korg and Blarek set off toward the medical center that houses the infirmary, while Evander and Angelica continue their way to the sparring area.

Anglica makes a comment with a smile, "Those two were definitely made for each other, and they do make a good couple."

Evander smiles at Anglica and continues walking.

~~~~~~~~~~~~~~~

Ten-minutes later, Blarek and Kal'korg arrive at the Infirmary, where the doctor, Ka'eel Isa, from the planet Fek'kat, raises an eyebrow and her amethyst eyes widen in alarm behind her large spectacles upon seeing them. Crossing her arms across her slender frame she asks, "And what have we here?" She examines Blarek with a disapproving shake of her head. "Let me guess, you got into another fight, and once again, I have to fix what's broken, hmm?" Frustrated, she inquires, "So how did it get started this time?"

Blarek mumbles his response, prompting a nod of understanding from the doctor. Kal'korg looks astonished. "You can understand what he's saying?" he asks in disbelief.

Doctor Isa looks at him blankly and replies, "Yes, I can. Not only am I a doctor, but I am also this world's foremost expert on the language of gibberish!"

Blarek rolls his eyes and points at his mouth. "Oh, she was being sarcastic," says Kal'korg, finally understanding.

The doctor directs her gaze toward Kal'korg. "Don't need to be a Gjargin to see his mouth is glued," she states matter-of-factly. She then places a cloth over Blarek's mouth, which startles him, and she gently dabs it with a special solution to dissolve the glue. "Now, for the love of stars, quit getting into so much mischief. One of these times, you're going to get so badly injured that it will take more than a simple warm soapy cloth and medical supplies to help you," she warns.

Blarek responds in gratitude. "Thank you again, Doc. And don't worry, you won't be seeing us for a long time. In fact, you could say you'll miss us because we've been gone so long," he quipped.

With a raised eyebrow and in a low tone, the doctor replies, "I doubt it. Knowing you two, I'll be seeing you both in here by the end of the week again. Now, good day."

Doctor Isa escorts them out of the infirmary, and Kal'korg can't resist teasing Blarek. "At least now you can go and have your snack, you big baby," he remarks.

Blarek glares at him and playfully smacks Kal'korg on the behind. "I don't deny it. Anyway, we better hurry up or we'll be late for our first officer duty," Blarek replies. Glancing at the holographic time display overhead, he exclaims, "Oh crap, we're going to be late for sure! We better book it over there!" Panicking, he adds, "We only have five minutes to get to the other side of the base! It's going to take us triple that at least to get there!"

Blarek and Kal'korg start running, and Doctor Isa peers out of her office. "Those two are going to be the death of each other, I swear," she mutters, taking a deep breath. "Quit running down the halls, you knuckleheads!" she shouts as they look back. They don't notice a scientist coming down the hall carrying a large box of graviton models, and they collide with him. Doctor Isa sighs and mutters to herself, "I might as well just stay with them the entire time they're here at this base." Before heading back into the infirmary, she stops and watches them both leave, wondering how two species with such different personalities could get along. As far as she knows, a male Pheonian is typically aggressive and fierce. While a male Ho'grenian is always alert, but timid. She then turns and goes back inside.

Meanwhile, Kal'korg and Blarek apologize to the scientist and help him pick up his belongings from the ground.

"We're so sorry, Professor Heligan. We didn't see you there," they say apologetically.

The professor, Enerson Heligan, a Nunkisian, is a friendly man with warm orange skin, dark teal hair, and a third eye located between his two eyebrows. Always easy going he was the federation's absent-minded professor. The professor grins and pats them on the head. Looking at the mess with his three yellow eyes he smiles and then turns back to the pair. "That's quite alright. At least none of the models broke, and you two will learn something from this experience," he reassures them.

Kal'korg and Blarek exchange glances and then turn back to the professor. "You mean looking where we're going?" Kal'korg asks.

The professor waves his hand dismissively. "No, I'm talking about how there is never a bad accident, unless it is a bad accident. In which case, why would I be smiling?" he chuckles. "Even though these models didn't break, do you not see how they got realigned?"

Both officers look perplexed by the professor's question. The professor takes out a mini device and scans the models, explaining how their alignment matters. After a few minutes of listening to him, the professor checks the time. "Oh my, look at the time. I better get going. Don't want to be late, now do I?" he says, gathering the rest of his things and walking down the hall. Blarek and Kal'korg are left in a daze by what they had just heard, and now they are late as well.

CHAPTER THREE

In the training center, Evander and Angelica are sparring using training swords. Angelica lands a hit across his head, prompting the Pheonian instructor to intervene. "Come on, Mr. Guryon, you have to keep your guard up. Try to anticipate where she is going to strike, block, and then execute a counter," the instructor advises Evander.

Determined to improve, Evander blocks another strike and launches a counterattack, only to be blocked by Angelica, who swiftly strikes him with a knee to the stomach. Wincing in pain, Evander falls to the mat and clutches his stomach.

"That's enough for now!" the instructor declares, approaching Evander and extending a helping hand says, "Mr. Guryon, you really have to learn how to counter attacks better, or you might get seriously hurt if you ever get into a fight. And as for you, Ms. Tenah... great job as usual on your sword handling and counterattacks. Your techniques excel every time I see you. Very impressive."

As the instructor walks away, he declares, "That's enough for the day. Some of you still need to practice more," and his gaze settles on Evander. "Some more than others. Now, off to the showers with you and get some rest. A well-rested mind and body are prepared for any task ahead. Remember this."

Evander heads toward the locker room to clean up, but he can't escape the ridicule and cruel name-calling from some of his fellow officers. Although he is typically a pacifist, Evander can't help but feel anger growing inside him. Cruel ideas for revenge cross his mind.

Angelica notices his growing anger and tries to calm him down. "Come on, Evan. Just ignore them. They're only trying to rile you up for their own amusement," Angelica reassures him. "Besides, why let them get to you now and not when they tossed a drink can at your head?" Evander simply shrugs and proceeds to the showers, determined to let go of the negativity.

After taking a shower, Evander heads outside and bumps into his girlfriend, Kes. "Hey, wonderful, how's your day going so far?" Kes asks, smiling up at Evander.

Kes, short for Kesaria, is Evander's father's lab assistant. Evander and Kes started dating right after he joined the UPF. Kes is an Aphrendite, a species known for their brilliance in mathematics and science. Her species has a very human-like appearance, with the exception that they have a tail, and their skin typically ranges from sky-blue to dark blue. Kes has dark sky-blue skin, is thin, medium height and has shoulder length emerald-green hair. Evander still doesn't know what Kes sees in him, but he is definitely amazed by her brilliance.

Evander replies with a shrug, "Could have gone worse, and seeing you always makes my day better." They laugh together and walk toward the mess hall, where they meet up with Blarek, Kal'korg, and Angelica. Evander waves at them and asks, "Hey, guys, what's cooking?"

Blarek and Kal'korg speak simultaneously, "Hey, Evan, doing great." Kal'korg takes a bite of his dinner and adds, "And look, his mouth isn't glued shut. More kisses for me and more headaches from listening to him talk non-stop."

Blarek laughs and playfully nudges Kal'korg on the shoulder. Rolling his eyes, he says, "I don't talk that much. Anyway, Evan, how did your training go?"

As they sit down, Evander replies, "It went well. Ange beat me up, but I guess that isn't new."

Angelica shakes her head and says, "I didn't beat you up. I just won and proved that I was better at it than you were."

Kes looks at Evander and reassures him, "Well, as long as you didn't harm my Evander too badly, that's the important thing, isn't it, Angelica?"

Angelica sets down her fork and takes a sip of her drink before replying, "Yes, it is, Kes. But don't sweat it. It was only practice, and I wouldn't let any real harm come to him."

Both Kes and Angelica stare at each other intently, creating a tense atmosphere.

Blarek can't help but giggle, "Why don't you two just have a make-out session right now? Evan here might enjoy that more than seeing you two fight."

Blarek's comment causes Kes and Angelica to turn their gazes directly at him, making him sink in his chair. Sensing the tension, Evander promptly suggests that he and Kes take a walk since it was a nice evening. Kes agrees and they head toward the garden area outside.

After they leave, Angelica's face turns red with anger as she mutters, "What does he see in her? She may seem all sweet and such, but I don't trust her at all."

Kal'korg tries to calm her down, saying, "Ange, I don't understand what's not to like about her. If I didn't know better, I would say you're just jealous of her and Evan's relationship."

Blarek sinks low in his seat, anticipating what is about to come. Angelica responds, "Jealous of that? How could I be jealous of her and Evan's relationship? Are you implying that I like Evander? He and I are just friends, and that is all, no more." Taking a deep breath and another sip of her drink, Angelica begins to calm down. "Still, though... what if I did like him more than that? Not that he would share my feelings about it. After all, he's got her!"

Blarek and Kal'korg sit there silently, contemplating what to say next.

Angelica continues eating the rest of her supper. She adds, "And another thing, I doubt we would even hit it off. He's more of a brother to me than anything else." She picks up her tray and says, "I'm heading to bed, and sorry, Kal'korg and Blarek, for losing my temper with both of you. Good night."

Kal'korg and Blarek wave and bid Angelica good night as she leaves.

While sitting on a bench near the fountain, Evander and Kes talk about their day. Kes holds Evander tight and asks how things are going and if he has caused any trouble.

Evander chuckles and replies, "No, I haven't gotten into any trouble. But Kal and Blarek, on the other hand, had a run-in with your brother, Jalerg, who apparently glued Blarek's mouth shut."

Kes shakes her head and sighs. "Yeah, I heard about that from him. But that's just who Jalerg is. I keep telling him he's going to get court-martialed one day, but he just shrugs it off."

Evander lets out a little laugh and says, "Yeah, that sounds like Jalerg. So, how are things going down at the lab? Making any progress with the new mechanized soldier?"

Kissing him on the cheek, Kes replies confidently, "You better believe it. We're almost done with the AI program. It's going to be the most advanced one yet and way better than any other model out there." She looks smug, as if she has discovered the cure for every known disease. "It's going to be your father's most brilliant invention yet, and of course, integrating it perfectly into a biological computer chip will be an even greater feat."

Evander listens intently, finding the whole project fascinating. The rest of the evening seems to slip by as they discuss the details of the project and how it is all coming together. Evander can't help but be mesmerized listening to her speak. To him, she has the voice of an angel. He is captivated with everything about her, from the way she smiles, to the way she talks, even the way her eyes look when talking about her work. There are only two other people he knows that share the same passion, his late mother and his dad.

Suddenly, Kes glances at the time and exclaims, "Oh damn, look at the time. You'd better get some rest for tomorrow. You're getting your first mission briefing in the morning, aren't you?"

Snapping back to the present, he glances at the time as well. "Crap, sorry. I guess I didn't want our moment to end." Laughing, he holds her hand over his, feeling a strong connection.

She looks at him with a gaze full of longing and says, "Well, I wouldn't mind staying here with you, but it's getting late, and it's getting colder outside." They both stand up from the bench, knowing it's time to head back to their respective living quarters. "Besides," Kes continues, "I have to go back to the lab. Your father is working late tonight, and he thinks he might have come up with a solution to a minor problem we've been having with the inter-matrix system of the sub-processor of the organic brain."

Evander's excitement rises, and he doesn't want the night to end. "Well, perhaps I can come with you and give both of you a hand?"

Kes reaches up and brings her lips to his. He wraps his hands around her waist and pulls her in closer. She wraps her hands around his neck and leans in to deepen the kiss. As Evan reaches his hand up her back and through her hair Kes pushes him away, saying, "Good night, Evan." Then she turns and walks away toward the science lab, leaving him feeling a bit disappointed.

Evander reluctantly makes his way to his living quarters, the thought of food not even crossing his mind. However, as he arrives at his doorstep, he notices a tray and a note waiting for him. Evander reads the note left by Angelica and a warm smile spreads across his face. He appreciates her thoughtfulness and the care she has shown him. It reminds him of the strong bond they share as friends and comrades. He feels a sense of comfort knowing that she is looking out for him, just like a sister would.

The note reads:

"Evan, I noticed you didn't grab anything to eat when you got to the mess hall, so I asked the cook to make something for you. By the time you get around to eating this, it will most probably be cold, but it's still better than nothing at all. You need your strength for your first mission briefing tomorrow. Also, remember you still have to get your uniform and ULTRA Suit. And don't forget to grab Blarek tomorrow, we both know how he will sometimes sleep in. Anyways,

*we'll talk more about it tomorrow, for now, just eat, sleep, and I'll
see you tomorrow.*

Ange"

Evander carefully places the note into his pocket and carries the
tray into his living quarters. He commands the door to open, and it
obediently slides open. Once inside, he sets the tray on his desk and
takes a seat. As he enjoys the meal Angelica arranged for him, his
mind starts to wander.

Thoughts of the upcoming mission blend with the conversation he
had with Kes earlier. The possibilities of the advanced mechanized
soldiers and their potential impact on the frontlines consume his
thoughts. But then, a deeper question arises—what if these soldiers
develop their own identity? Could it jeopardize the principles and
values of the UPF? Evander shakes off the intense contemplation and
refocuses on his meal, eagerly anticipating the mission that awaits
him.

With a sense of excitement, Evander reflects on his journey so far.
He dreams of one day becoming a captain and leading his own crew,
issuing commands and making a difference. Lost in his daydream, he
swings an imaginary sword, fires an imaginary pistol, and envisions
himself as a hero for the federation.

Caught up in his imaginary adventure, Evander accidentally knocks over a picture frame of his mother. The memories come rushing back—the day she died in the tragic accident at the facility where she worked. He recalls visiting her in the infirmary, her final words urging him to care for his father and reminding him that he is their own created universe. The pain of losing her resurfaces, and a solitary tear rolls down his cheek.

He can recall the last words she said to him before passing away "Evan, be brave, be kind, but above all else, be your own star!"

Staring at his reflection in the mirror, Evander sees a mixture of determination and longing. He envisions a world where his mother is still alive, proud of his achievements and his decision to join the Star division. With a heavy heart, he sets the picture of his mother back in its place and prepares for bed. He says the command "lights out," and the room darkens. As he lies down, a glimmer of moonlight illuminates the picture and casts a gentle light on his face.

Tomorrow is a new day, filled with possibilities and challenges. Evander drifts off to sleep, holding his mother's memory close to his heart and feeling a renewed sense of purpose in his journey within the UPF.

CHAPTER FOUR

Later that night, with twin moons shimmering down on a lab building, Kes is walking briskly toward it. She suddenly gets an uneasy sense of being followed, when she turns around however, she doesn't see anyone, so she continues walking. She finally arrives at the lab and upon entering, she sees Evander's father, Doctor Guryon, asleep at the computer desk.

Looking at the diagram schematic on the screen board behind him, she can see that he's had a breakthrough with one of the projects he's been working on. She continues walking through the lab. Noticing some of the test subjects being built and grown in a chamber: metallic skeleton structures being produced with living tissue, infused with graphene and synthetic Gongorian spider silk being graphed onto it.

Getting to her station, she begins testing the upload process of an experimental new AI onto a few biochips. The computer indicates that the whole thing will take several hours to transfer. With that, she goes over to Doctor Guryon's desk and wakes him. Gently nudging him "Doctor... Doctor... I just initiated the test uploads into a few biochips, as you requested of me earlier. Shall I go and prepare a few more, just in case?"

The doctor rubs his eyes, takes a sip of his cold coffee and replies, "That would be good." The doctor looks around, disoriented, and asks Kes, "By the way, what time is it? And where are my glasses?"

"They're on top of your head, Doctor," Kes replies. "Also, the time is 2300 hours."

Pulling his glasses down, he says, "Thank you Kes. At least I got a few more hours of sleep."

"Yes Doctor," Kes replies and goes off to prepare more biochips.

Doctor Guryon calls over another lab assistant to help him check on the chambers to see how they are progressing. Noticing a few fluctuations in the readings on the side of one, he decides to peer inside the chamber, making sure the graphing of the biological tissue was taking hold on the nano tubular skeletal structure. He asks his assistant to verify his readings, but everything seems to check out fine. It could be normal statistical outliers, but he requests his assistant to keep an eye on the readings, just in case.

Making his way to Kes' station, Doctor Guryon asks, "What's the ETA on those biochips, just so I know that we're on schedule?"

"The computer states that it should take at least a few hours, sir. Shall I go and help with checking on the rest of the chambers?" Kes inquires.

"Thank you Kes, that would be appreciated. While you're at it, make sure there isn't any more fluctuations with the rest of them, please. Hate to have to dispose of the batch due to faulty readings." Doctor Guryon states hoping that the anomaly was just that one time. Kes agrees and leaves to check the other chambers.

Another lab assistant comes up to the Doctor with a message from High Command. "Excuse me sir, but the High Command wishes to know how things are coming along with your upgrades to the ULTRA suit. What should I tell them?"

Doctor Guryon just shakes his head and asks, "Don't those people sleep?" The assistant insists that High Command needs an answer right away. "Just tell them I'm still getting the bugs out of the prototype and it should be ready in 3 months." He lets out a sigh, thinking to himself, "I wish they'd understand that things like this take time." He takes another sip from his cold coffee and heads back to his desk.

The assistant informs High Command. Dissatisfied with the response they order him to put them on the viewing screen. The Doctor looks up, startled, as an admiral's voice comes over the speaker, "Doctor Guryon, we expect results a bit quicker than this. We understand that you have other projects on the go, but we expected more results sooner than this with the upgrades. What's the delay?"

Doctor Guryon nudges his glasses up. "Well, you see Admirals and Madam Galactic President, we hit a snag of sorts with this particular AI program." He clears his throat and continues, "The nanobots themselves are functioning with rudimentary programing, but creating a specific AI for them has . . . well, unforeseen setbacks."

They just blankly stare at him, and with a wave of the President's hand, she ushers everyone in the area to leave. Kes, ducks around the corner and listens in. "What sort of setbacks are we talking about here?" asks one of the admirals.

"Well, Admiral Elagal, it appears whenever we tried putting the AI into the shared matrix mind, it develops a completely different type of personality than the one we made for it, almost at random." Doctor Guryon says while inputting the algorithmic code for the AI program, so the admirals and the president can see. "You see here, this is how it should look but watch what happens when we put it into the matrix mind."

He begins to download the program into the nanobots, which at first glance seems fine, but suddenly the nanobots begin to speak in unison "Hey h-hey there Admiral s-squidy face, how's it go-go-going?"

The nanobots then morph into a small stove and then into a small hat rack, finally into a miniature jackhammer "W-w-e are s-s-s-o-o-o plea-se-d to be at y-ou-r se-rv . . ."

Doctor Guryon quickly turns the AI off and turns to the screen, "Sir, as you can see, that's what I was talking about. We're having difficulties locating the malfunctioning code. It has taken us years to get it this far. We estimate the completion of this particular project to be done at least within three more months, if not more."

Kes, knowing all about the setbacks, and not wanting to be witness to any scrutiny the Doctor might face, walks off.

Looking upset with the news, one admiral questions why it morphs into smaller versions of certain objects. "Well, you see Admiral La'rein, the nanobots are capable of mimicking things, but only at a smaller scale, because…the nanobots themselves only have so much of their own material. If they wanted to take on a bigger or the same size of a certain item, they will need to absorb materials from their surroundings, which they are capable of doing." Picking up a small can, the doctor turns on the nano-bots without the AI and attempts to have the nanobots absorb and morph into something of a more proportionate size, which they do and for a few moments, did so without issue. "As you can see, sir, the nanobots absorbed and are able to mimic an object of its exact size." The nanobots suddenly start to hiccup and then regurgitate the material it absorbed.

Doctor Guryon looks disappointed, but turns to face the screen and explains, "But as you can tell, we still have a few glitches to work out, even with the AI turned off."

Dissatisfied with the experiment, the admirals tell Doctor Guryon to try to isolate the problem and fix it, or to start looking for a different position, and end the transmission. Doctor Guryon walks over to his office and sits in his desk to think about the situation at hand. "Dammit! What am I going to do? I've got so many projects that they've given me to get done and very little time. I wish they understood how important it is to have time to work on these things." He turns on a second monitor and begins to work again on trying to figure out the issue with the coding.

Hours later, Kes is back at her station entering in the few last lines of code for a different project they are working on. Suddenly she hears something! It sounds like a faint whisper from a disembodied voice. She looks around and can't see anyone else around. Looking out she sees Doctor Guryon is still at his desk looking worried and there is no one else around. Kes just shrugs it off as lack of sleep, but she hears it again. She looks around some more and asks, "Is someone there?" She hears the whisper again, but this time louder and clearer.

"Yes, I am your conscience, and I say you are still a snaerk with no bite!" A disembodied voice sarcastically whispers into Kes's ear.

Kes immediately realizes whose voice it is and says, "Jalerg, you shit-head, stop that at once! I'm working on a very important project and the Doctor was just given an ultimatum." Kes expects Jalerg to come out from some hiding place, but to her surprise he simply becomes visible!

Laughing, Jalerg says, "You guys sure have nice things! Mind if I keep this cloaking watch?"

Kes grabs it out of his hands and angrily tells him, "No! What are you even doing here and at this time of night? It's 2:15 am!"

Jalerg just giggles some more and says, "Oh you know, I got bored with terrorizing some of the newbies in this place." Hopping onto the desk, he looks straight at his sister with a smirk. "Being able to spy on the fine women getting undressed was a definite perk!" Gleefully pointing at the object in Kes's hand he says, "That watch was SO handy for that, you sure I can't keep it?"

Kes frustratingly smacks him across his head and places the watch out of reach. "A—you're sick AND I'm still surprised you're still able to be here and B—yes I am definitely DAMN sure you can't have the watch back, pervert!" Jalerg tries to beg for it to no avail.

Kes goes back to her programing while Jalerg hovers around her. "So, what's that you're working on now?" Kes just tries to ignore him. Jalerg persists. "Come on tell me, you know I won't leave you alone!"

Kes grumbles "Fine I'll tell you what I'm working on…"

Jalerg cuts her off, "Well, I'm bored already. See you around sis!"

Kes vexed and annoyed, "What the hell? Why are you even here? And why ask me something you didn't want to know?"

Jalerg smiles and says, "I was curious as to how far done you were with your project and I felt like annoying you, that's all!"

"Just go away so I can get back to work!" Kes says angrily.

Jalerg just laughs, while slyly putting the cloaking watch in his pocket. "Whatever you say sis. I'll catch you around."

As Jalerg leaves, Kes notices the watch gone and yells, "JALERG!"

Doctor Guryon rushes out of his office. "What is going on out here Kes?" he asks.

Kes, being too embarrassed to admit that her brother came and stole the watch, says, "Nothing…" Kes tried to quickly think up a good excuse "I'm just mad at Jalerg for always picking on Evander and his friends. It makes me look bad being related to him."

Doctor Guryon shakes his head and says, "Well, don't let it get to you. You can't help who your family is, or what they do. Now, please, no more interruptions." He heads back into his office.

Kes goes back to coding but is distracted by thoughts of how to get the watch back from her stupid brother.

CHAPTER FIVE

That same night, Jalerg puts the watch on and begins sneaking into the women's barracks. While looking around, he notices one of the officer trainees, Cadet Nylara. Curious as to what she is doing at this late hour, he starts to follow her. Jalerg notices that she is one of the nocturnal species. He is always attracted to their type and watches where she goes. He figures he hit the jackpot, because she goes into the ladies' showers. He quickly slips through the door before it closes.

After following her in, he observes her, as she gets undressed and steps into the shower stall. He watches her gently gliding her wings out of her uniform and letting down her green hair. Her magenta-coloured skin is glistening, as she steps into the shower. Jalerg begins to salivate at the sight of her slender build with luscious curves at just the right places.

She turns quickly in his direction, like an eagle seeing their prey and calls out, "I know you're out there, I can hear you. I may not see you directly, but I can definitely hear your breathing and your heartbeat. I'm a Betlarian, which means my hearing is very acute."

Jalerg wipes his mouth and tries to hold his breath and slow his heartbeat, but Nylara turns the shower off, wraps a towel around herself, and begins heading toward her locker.

Jalerg, thinking that he still has a chance to further study the beautiful cadet, tries to sneak up behind her. To his sudden dismay, she turns around and sprays a sour mist from her mouth, into his eyes, and runs for the exit. Jalerg screams but quickly regains his composure and thinks, *"Shit! I'm going to get into trouble for sure!"* He runs after Nylara, who frantically tries to open the door. Jalerg, however, quickly whips her face with his tail, dazing her. Not knowing what and where the offending object came from, she turns around and runs toward the rear entrance. But before she can get there, she slips on the wet floor, hits her head on the side of a bench, and is knocked out. Jalerg, now more worried than before, starts to panic. He lifts her body and drapes her over his shoulder. Then, increasing the range of invisibility to encompass her as well, Jalerg opens the door to the ladies' showers and leaves, hoping to take her to a secure location while she is still unconscious.

Jalerg runs as fast as he can with a limp cadet draped over his shoulder, arms and head dangling down his back. His pace is slowed from the weight of the cadet, and he keeps stumbling whenever he gets too close to the edge of the pathway, tripping over the jagged rocks placed there. Too late to react, Jalerg receives a punch to his kidneys—Nylara has woken up.

With the cadet writhing frantically he, tightens his grip on her and is rewarded with a knee to his chest. Suddenly, she begins to scream and in a state of panic Jalerg covers her mouth with his tail and in a whisper says, "Be quiet, I'm already in enough trouble as it is, without you making things worse for me!" She groans and bites his tail as hard as she can. With an angry yelp, Jalerg throws the cadet hard to the ground and kicks her in a reflexive motion. He hears a loud crack as her head is slammed into one of the sharp rocks. He suddenly hears someone scream and turns, seeing people coming to see what the commotion was about. He looks down and sees that the watch has dropped off making him visible. Nylara is lying naked and twisted on the ground with her head shattered, bright purple blood pooling on the path below his feet, and the towel lying a foot away. Jalerg grabs the watch and breaks out into a run, getting as far away from the dead cadet, and the growing crowd, as quickly as he can.

~~~~~~~~~~~~~~~

Kes hears footsteps and looks up from her coding. Three security guards are approaching with grim looks on their faces. They inform her that her brother was spotted killing a fellow cadet and fled the scene. One of the security members ask urgently "Do you have any idea where he might be hiding out?"

Kes, shaken up from the news, answered, "I don't know, I swear." The security guards looked grim and even a bit accusatory. She added, "There is one spot he might...." Kes is interrupted by a loud explosion in the distance. They all turn and rush to the viewing port just in time to see a ship flying away.

The meanest looking of the three officers turns to the other two and says, "You two go check it out, and make sure that wasn't Jalerg on that ship." As the two security officers nod their head in acknowledgement and turn away, the head security officer returns his attention to Kes and asks, "What were you about to say?"

Kes, looking dumbstruck, says, "I was going to say, the one spot he might be is in an abandoned weapons testing area."

The security officer takes one step forward and says, "Come with me. We'll go and check it out. Hopefully he is there and not on that ship!" Kes nods weakly and leaves with the officer.

A few moments later Doctor Guryon comes out of the office, looks around, and asks, "Kes, are you there?" Looking puzzled he says to himself, "I could have sworn I heard her still here. I must have dreamt it…OH NO! I MUST HAVE FALLEN ASLEEP AGAIN!" Doctor Guryon rushes back into his office and goes back to his work.

A half hour later Kes and the security officer arrive at the abandoned building. They gaze up at a 100 foot building with two side buildings. All three domed rooftops are crumbling, with the siding oxidized. As they step inside, the officer remarks, "I'm surprised this place is even still up." He pauses to turn on his built-in shoulder lights and starts looking around.

"It stopped being used only 5 years ago after that horrendous explosion…" Kes replies while also looking around using her wrist light.

The officer then asks, "Wasn't that the one the good Doc's wife was involved in?"

"The very one," Kes replies solemnly.

A sudden noise grabs Kes' attention, and she turns quickly toward the sound. Suddenly, plasma shots are fired, and the officer falls down to the ground screaming in pain. Kes rushes over to him and is relieved to find he was only wounded, although very severely. "JALERG! YOU BRAINLESS IDIOT!" Kes screams at the top of her lungs, with no reply. Kes hurriedly wraps the officer's wound with a bandage from his first aid pouch. Another noise startles her and, as she looks around the corner, she sees a silhouette of a person. Thinking she knows who it is, she sneaks around, only to find a targeting dummy.

The officer yells, "Kes, did you find anything?"

Kes yells back, "The only thing I found is the wrong dummy!" She then hears more rustling and calls out, "Jalerg—this isn't funny. You're in real trouble this time and there's no turning back. Listen to your big sister and turn yourself in. Perhaps you'll get a fair reduced sentence." Kes still hears no response, which at this point is starting to piss her off.

"JALERG!" Kes screams again. Then it hits her, he must be using the cloaking watch. She heads back to the officer and asks if she can use his flash pellet grenades and his badge communicator. She informs him that she's making an EMP explosive with the communicator to try and flush out Jalerg from his hiding place. When he's revealed she'll use the pellets to stun him for a bit. The officer agrees and she proceeds on making the device. Several moments later it's built and Kes tosses the explosive in the middle of the firing range. Kes notices a figure in the middle of the smoky haze, and she throws the pellet grenades, and then starts running in the attempt to tackle it to the ground. It topples over with a clank and Kes looks down to see an old robot Jalerg modified, holding a gun.

Watching the scene the officer asks, "Where's Jalerg?"

"Jalerg must have been here, placed the gun into the robot's hand, and programmed it to shoot at anyone that wasn't him," Kes answers angrily.

"Damn! That means it was him on that ship then!" the officer responded, pounding his fist into the ground. The officer gets up and Kes rushes over to help him. Angrily, the officer grumbles, "Here I was hoping this was going to be easy. I guess not."

~~~~~~~~~~~~~~~~

Back at the lab Doctor Guryon comes out of his office, just as Kes walks back in with the wounded security officer in tow. The doctor exclaims, "Please tell me I'm dreaming and that you aren't bringing a wounded person into our lab. Then again, I hope I'm not dreaming, because otherwise I'll be mad at myself again when I wake up…"

Kes interrupts, "I thought you might have heard the commotion from before. My idiot brother is wanted by security for murdering a cadet."

Doctor Guryon nearly drops his coffee cup. "DAMN IT!" Both Kes and the officer look at the doctor perplexed. He exclaims harshly, "I was hoping I was dreaming! Well, don't just stand there Kes! We're not the hospital or the nurse's office, but we're the next best thing, go grab that dermal putty and the handheld re-generator."

Kes quickly does what she was told and hands the items to the doctor. The officer asks, "What's that gunk for?"

With a raised eyebrow the doctor responds, "This is a synthetic polymorphic compound that is able to mimic any living thing's tissue and cells, allowing for faster healing no matter the species. And with the help of the re-generator, this should heal up in no time."

Looking confused the officer replies, "I have no clue what you just said, but you're the expert, so I trust you."

The Doctor smiles, "Good to hear, because you're the first to test it." The officer's face goes pale and looks shocked. Kes watches Doctor Guryon remove the bandage, exposing a burnt wound and the muscle underneath. He applies the special putty compound onto the officer's wound and says, "This man is lucky that the weapon used wasn't one with projectiles, but one with a narrow, yet weak laser. This cauterized the wound. But the entire layer of the epidermis down to the muscle was damaged." The Doctor then turns on the re-generator, aiming it at the wound. The compound quickly starts repairing the lost tissue, acting like a skin graft. The colour of the putty changes to match the officer's skin tone and the wound is then healed. What seems to Kes like only a minute or two later, the Doctor looks up and says, "There, all done! And it was a success! How do you feel?"

Sitting up, the officer states, "Feels much better. Thanks Doc!"

Doctor Guryon gives him a satisfied look and says, "You're welcome, and thank you for being the first test subject."

Kes taps Doctor Guryon on the shoulder and asks, "Is it alright, if I leave for the rest of the night? It's almost 5:00 AM and I don't feel all that great."

Doctor Guryon says sympathetically, "Very understandable Ms. Kyrandor. After what you just found out and what transpired, I wouldn't blame you one bit for being a bit shaken up over it."

"Thank you, Doctor," Kes replies and then turns and heads toward the exit of the laboratory. Once outside, she starts walking the bush-lined path to her building. Suddenly a tail clamps itself against her mouth and two hands wrap themselves around her waist. She feels herself being dragged behind some bushes near her building. Kes's eyes widen in shock when she is turned around and sees that it was Jalerg. He removes his tail from over her mouth and she nearly screams, "YOU…"

Jalerg quickly covers her mouth again and tells her to keep it down. "Look I didn't mean to kill that girl. It was a complete accident. Please, you got to help me get out of this."

Kes takes a step back and looks around to see if the security officer was following her or if anyone else was around. After confirming that they were alone, she whispers, "Just leave! I'm not putting my career in jeopardy just to help you. You killed someone, you moron! And if I help you then I'd be an accomplice to it! The work I'm doing here is far too important to me to put myself at risk for you!"

Jalerg frowns angrily and says, "Fine! If you won't help, then I'm on my own. You can keep your precious career intact, but I'll remember this whenever you need help."

Kes scoffs at the notion and says, "If I need help, I've got someone else to turn to!"

Jalerg laughs and says, "He can't help—right now he can't even help himself!"

Kes turns and begins to walk away, saying, "I wouldn't underestimate him if I were you Jalerg. I'll pretend I didn't see you, but that's as much help as you're getting from me!"

Jalerg doesn't bother to respond. He puts the cloaking watch back on, looks around and skulks away.

~~~~~~~~~~~~

Early the next morning, an announcement is made over the speakers throughout the UPF headquarters. "Attention all junior officers! You are to report to briefing room 918! Repeat: junior officers, briefing room 918!" Evander looks up from his breakfast and asks, "I wonder what they have for our first time out?"

Angelica smiles, "Probably something easy, like going to Bel'rurian and helping the senior people."

CHAPTER SIX

Evander and Angelica walk toward the briefing room, with Blarek and Kal'korg walking hand-in-hand behind them. They sit down in the briefing room to join the rest of the assembled group to wait for Commander Drixen and get their assignments. Much to everyone's surprise it isn't Drixen that walks up to the front of the room. Admiral Sarklak, the senior officer in charge of the entire UPF headquarters, a fierce looking Alnilamian, marches up to the front of the briefing room with a harsh and determined look on his face. "OK OFFICERS, THIS ASSIGNMENT JUST CAME IN! THERE HAS BEEN A MURDER ON CAMPUS AND A SUSPECTED RAPE! SOMEONE CAME ON OUR BASE AND KILLED ONE OF THE NIGHTTIME CADETS! THE PERSON IN QUESTION IS JALERG KYRANDOR!" Both Angelica and Evander side glanced each other with shock.

Angelica and Evander side-glance at each other in shock. The admiral continues, "KYRANDOR HAS BEEN REPORTED TO HAVE LEFT THE BASE LESS THAN TWO HOURS AGO AND HAS BEEN TRACKED TO THE PLANET B'OWREN. YOUR MISSION IS SIMPLE! YOU ARE TO TAKE ONE OF OUR CHASER SHIPS AND APPREHEND THIS CRIMINAL AND BRING HIM TO JUSTICE! I KNOW HE KILLED ONE OF OUR OWN AND I KNOW YOU'LL WANT TO DO EVERYTHING

YOU CAN TO BRING HIM IN! BUT REMEMBER, FIRST AND
FOREMOST IS, WE ALWAYS BRING PEOPLE IN ALIVE!
LEADING THIS MISSION WILL BE LIEUTENANT ANGELICA
TENAH! TENAH, YOU WILL COME SEE ME IMMEDIATELY
IN MY OFFICE AND I SHALL GIVE YOU THE FULL
BRIEFING. IS THAT CLEAR?"

Angelica looks up, "YES SIR!"

The admiral dismisses everyone to get back to work. Angelica
tells Evander she will catch up with them later after her briefing with
the admiral. Evander, along with Blarek and Kal'korg, are walking
toward the ship bay when someone rushes toward Kal'korg. "Excuse
me sir, but Doctor Isa is requesting your assistance with a project of
hers and was wondering if you could give her a hand with it."

Kal'korg looks confused. "I'm pretty certain she's got me
confused with someone else. I'm not that knowledgeable in lab
stuff."

The young apprentice shakes his head's. "No, I'm certain she was
asking for you. She said to go get Kal'korg, he looks like a green-
furred lion and a little de-shuffled."

Evander and Blarek couldn't help but laugh a little, while
Kal'korg just shrugs, with the look of embarrassment. "Okay, I'll be

right there. I'll catch up with you guys at the ship bay." Evander and Blarek head off toward the bay to prepare for the mission ahead.

~~~~~~~~~~~~~

Meanwhile, Angelica is getting a quick briefing from the admiral. "Lieutenant, I would have stated this in front of the rest of the group, but the information I'm about to share with you is sensitive, considering the subject is the brother of the girlfriend of one of your closest companions."

Angelica responds in agreement. "That would be Evander Guryon sir, but why would you think he shouldn't know this?"

The admiral sits down and motions Angelica to do the same. "You see, Jalerg made off with some sensitive tech from Doctor Guryon's lab and with Ms. Kyrandor being one of his father's lab assistants, I feel he might take this a bit too personal." Admiral Sarklak leans back in his seat. "You see, with the recent passing of Ensign Guryon's mother, in that HORRIBLE lab accident…"

Angelica cuts him off, "You mean the accident that still isn't solved?"

The admiral continues, "That's correct, we still don't have all the pieces of it, but seeing as how his father is working with tech and other government projects and how things could have gone worst, I feel it might dredge up the ensign's bad memories and end up causing him to not be affective at his job."

Angelica looks at the admiral puzzled. "I still don't quite understand why you don't want him to know, I get that Jalerg is Kes's brother, but it's not like there's a love loss relationship with him or Evander. Even Kes can't stan…"

The admiral interrupts and leans forward toward Angelica, "Kesaria has also become a suspect. Someone claims to have seen her talking to her brother shortly before his escape from the base. We don't want Evander to know that we're also looking into her as well. That's where you come in." Sarklak takes a deep breath in and explains, "We suspect that there is someone else pulling the strings in the technology theft. When you catch Jalerg today, I don't trust him to tell you the truth behind what is going on. Hence, I want you to investigate Kesaria, to make sure she's still on the up and up, so to speak."

Angelica is dumbstruck and hardly believes Kes can be a suspect in a murder. She may not like Kes very much, but she never pegged her as the criminal type. The admiral dismisses Angelica, commanding her not to say anything to Evander and to keep everything under wraps. She nods her head in acknowledgement and leaves his office.

Later, Angelica, catches up with Evander and Blarek. "Ange, what did the admiral say?" Evander asks.

"It's top secret, only captain's need to know. Sorry, nothing I can do!" She turns around to look at the UPF Star Cruiser, leaving Evander puzzled, but he just shrugs it off. Angelica then realizes "Wait! Where's Kal'korg?"

Just as she asks, Kal'korg runs up to the rest of them, "Sorry I'm late..." he takes a deep breath "...but Doctor Isa wanted my help..." still winded, he takes another breath "...with an experiment she was running," he finishes explaining, completely out of breath.

Blarek questions with concern, "What did she have you do? Run a marathon or something?"

Kal'korg shakes his head; while still trying to catch his breath, he takes a moment to regain his composure before answering. "She wanted me to test her new bionic legs and see if she could integrate them seamlessly with the ULTRA Suit. I just got on the treadmill when they started to malfunction." His colour started going back to the normal green. "The legs, though somewhat seamlessly integrated, wouldn't stop running and she had a heck of time trying to get them to stop!"

Angelica giggled a little and recovered her composure. "Well, a little exercise does you good. Thankfully you made it!"

Kal'korg's colour goes flushed again out of embarrassment. Evander pats him on his back, while Blarek hugs him and gently kisses him on the head.

All four friends, along with the rest of the crew, step onto their newly assigned ship, The UPF Star Cruiser. Angelica, along with Evander and Blarek, head to the command deck, while Kal'korg heads to the medical bay to check things out and have things organized to his liking. As mission captain, Angelica sits in the captain's chair where she can observe the entire operation. Although off mission she has the title of Lieutenant, within the scope of the mission, and inside the ship, her crew addresses her as Captain, namely to distinguish between her and the other officers on the ship of the same rank. Evander, having been assigned second in command, seats himself next to Angelica in the center of the command hub. As second, his primary responsibility is monitoring and scanning all external environments. Blarek, having been assigned co-pilot, seats himself next to Ensign P'thorkia, the ship's pilot. Blarek looks over at the ensign and gives her a friendly smile.

P'thorkia is from Mira, a planet with a slightly heavier gravity than Earth. She has pink skin with white stripes, completely black eyes, and tendrils for hair. P'thorkia returns Blarek's smile, timidly, and he can immediately tell that she is nervous about her first time flying a ship on assignment.

From her captain's seat, Angelica looks around. She has done so many simulations, preparing herself for this moment, but her heart is still racing as she prepares to lead her first command. She turns on the comms and makes a speech. "Everyone, this may be our first time going out on a mission together, but rest assured, I have complete faith in your abilities to accomplish our goal. We will succeed as long as we all remember what we learned from our academy days!" Taking a deep breath, she continues, "We will bring justice to our fallen compatriot. We will see a criminal brought in and detained. We shall not allow his villainy to permanently stain our reputation as protectors of peace. So please remember…WE ARE UPF AND WE WILL UPHOLD THE LAWS OF OUR UNIVERSE!" All throughout the ship everyone cheered and applauded.

Evander leans toward Angelica and whispers, "Excellent speech Captain. Now, let's go catch us a criminal."

Angelica punches in the coordinates for B'owren - the last known location of Jalerg Kyrandor. She then gives the command to Ensign P'thorkia to take the ship out of dock and to prepare for a dimensional-hop.

Blarek whispers to P'thorkia, "You know I never could wrap my head around how the DHD works exactly. I actually got that part of the entrance exam wrong. The only thing I know is that DHD stands for Dimensional Hop Drive." Ensign P'thorkia smiles weakly at Blarek, hesitating for a moment to familiarize herself with the controls.

Angelica looks expectantly at her, then asks, "Ensign P'thorkia, is there a problem?"

The ensign nervously responds "No captain, I'm just… I'm just familiarizing myself with the ship, first time flying a star class chaser ship, like this one, is all."

Angelica leans forward "You should be well-familiarized with all ships, especially this one, considering you were also given the manual ahead of time."

Ensign P'thorkia looks back at her in embarrassment and says, "Yes ma'am, sorry ma'am." She then presses a button, and the ship begins to move forward.

"Nice and easy P'thorkia, I don't want to damage the ship before we even get out of the launch center." Suddenly, the ship begins to rumble, and everyone starts to look around nervously.

Moments later an alarm starts going, and a person from engineering comes on the intercom on the bridge saying, "Captain, this is Lieutenant Commander Froslo from engineering."

Angelica responds with a sigh "What is it, Mr. Froslo?"

He then bellows out, "Tell the dodgy pilot to bloody-well take the goddamn parking brake off! The damn flippin' intake valves are bleedin' closed and are about to friggin' blow!"

Ensign P'thorkia's face turns from pink to bright red as she swipes down on the console to her side. Angelica presses the intercom for engineering and calmly says, "Thank you for that colourful reminder, Froslo. Next time I would suggest calling up without the swearing, thank you!" In the background she hears most of the engineers swearing up a storm and banging items around.

Evander leans in with a smirk, "You know better than to tell Calidorfians not to swear, especially ones that are engineers!" Evander has met several Calidorfians while he was in training. Their race is short, compared to most races in the fleet, with a medium build. They have red eyes like a gerbil's, brown short fur covering much of their body, and a nose like a dog's. Despite their rodent-like appearance, Calidorfians have played a crucial role in learning and disseminating human languages and culture. But the most distinguishing feature in Evander's opinion is their rough expression and even rougher language. I don't think he's ever had a conversation with one that hasn't included at least one swear word in each sentence.

Angelica regains her composure, and trying not to look flustered, says to the ensign again, "Shall we be off? Oh, and P'thorkia, this time without almost blowing up the ship?"

"Yes Captain," replies P'thorkia.

Blarek leans over to Ensign P'thorkia and whispers, "Can I give you some assistance?" P'thorkia nods discreetly at Blarek, and he enters in a series of commands to smoothly depart from the port.

As the ship swiftly moves away, Ensign P'thorkia leans over to Blarek and says quietly, "By the way, a DHD is a somewhat difficult thing to grasp, but the short version is, the drive itself is its own power supply, powered by an antimatter fusion drive." Keeping her eyes on the controls, she continues, "Once activated, the DH device fires out, at near light-speed, particles that collide in the front of an object, like our ship, just to cause a large enough wormhole in subspace, that can take you anywhere in the known universe."

Blarek smiles inwardly as P'thorkia's confidence visibly builds as she provides her explanation. Blarek remains confused but doesn't ask any more questions. As the tail end of the ship leaves the UPF base, and makes it through the planet's atmosphere, he punches in the command for the hop to the B'owren system and nods to Ensign P'thorkia. She presses a button and the drive engages. The process takes a mere few seconds when, in front of the ship, two barely visible blue dots collide. From the collision, a ship-sized passage forms within subspace that connects two distant points in space. The sound of the drive was almost angelic sounding, but with a mechanical tone to it. The ship goes through the wormhole, and they are instantly at a different point in space. Moments later, the wormhole closes behind them.

~~~~~~~~~~~~~~~~

Still wearing the cloaking watch, Jalerg sneaks into a high-tech facility to try and steal some other experimental technology that involves advanced creative AI. He's glad that the first thing that he stole for his employer was the watch - it is making his escape and subsequent thefts so much easier. Jared thinks to himself that once the cloaking technology becomes widespread, security is going to tighten. Right now, most of the laboratories still use camera technology to detect intruders, allowing himself to enter areas relatively undetected. Suddenly, Jared hears someone coming into the room he's in and quickly hides behind a desk. Although he is still wearing the watch, he knows that there's still a glimmer trace when bright direct lights hit him. He peers around the corner, cautiously, as to not be seen. He sees a security guard walking around to check on things in the room.

Jalerg quietly moves around to the opposite side of the room, nearly knocking over a beaker. The security guard looks in the direction of the noise but sees nothing, so he shrugs it off as nothing and leaves. Jalerg exhales the breath he doesn't realize he's holding, then proceeds to open the computer console and download specs relating to the AI program he's hired to steal. Suddenly, his communication badge vibrates. He ignores it, in a hurry to get the job finished. The badge vibrates again, so he finally answers it with a low but angry "What?" His face turns pale as he realizes who it is on the communications.

"You're being sloppy, even with that invisible tech watch!" a bellowing angry voice is heard through the earpiece. Jalerg's employer is keeping tabs on him. Trembling, Jalerg quickly tries to apologize. The voice interrupts, "I don't want to hear any more excuses from you! You were supposed to get in and get out, WITHOUT CAUSING A SCENE! I hired you for a series of simple thefts, and now I have to deal with a murder!" Jalerg just freezes and stays as silent as death itself.

Trying to regain his composure, Jalerg is able to say a few words, "I'm sorry, I just got caught up in the moment and…"

The angry voice, this time even louder, causes Jalerg to drop his communicator. To his horror, he can still hear the other person's voice, as though he was standing behind him. "YOU'RE NOT GOING TO WORM YOUR WAY OUT OF THIS! You're going to have to find a way to rectify this mess! Get your sister to help if needed. Bribe some of the officers as well. DO I MAKE MYSELF CLEAR!"

Before Jalerg can respond, communication is cut off. He picks up his communicator, trembling, and tries to regain his composure. He looks around, almost expecting to see that his employer was there the entire time but sees no one. Jalerg shakes his head in confusion, grabs the download, and leaves.

Above the planet, the UPF Star Cruiser arrives and begins circling in orbit. Evander begins to scan the planet below for Jalerg's life signs. Suddenly, he spots on his sensors a ship just leaving the atmosphere. Angelica instructs him to scan it to see if Jalerg's on board. As he does so, the ship suddenly explodes, the remnants crashing on a nearby moon. "Scan the wreckage Ensign Guryon, for

Jalerg's bio-signs - I need to know if he was on that ship," Angelica commands formally to Evan.

"The scans report a positive for Jalerg's bio-signs, Captain. There are no signs of life," replies Evan, equally formally.

"This makes no sense!" Angelica replies, mostly to herself. She commands again, "Re-scan the planet again, and include all surrounding areas. I am not satisfied that this is the end of Jalerg Kyrandor." Just as Evan begins to carry out her command, a second ship appears from the planet's surface and immediately initiates a dimensional-hop and disappears from view.

Angelica slams down on the arm rests, like a hammer hitting a nail. She gives the command to follow the ship before the wormhole closes. The ship accelerates and they manage to get through just before it closes. Suddenly multiple ships pop up on the sensors, with their weapons ready to fire. Angelica, in a startled tone, shouts, "ARM WEAPONS EVERYONE! SHIELDS UP AND BRACE FOR A FIGHT!"

Evan quickly punches in a communication to the medic bay that reads, "Kal'korg - heads up - we might be receiving injuries - get ready…"

All the ships start to fire simultaneously, but as each shot hits the ship nothing happens. The shields are not being affected. Evan scans the surrounding area and turns to Angelica and reports, startled, "Captain, the ships are only holograms!" He continues, "They are being projected by small satellites with signals telling us that we are drawing fire!"

"What the hell is happening!" Angelica continues angrily, "I've never heard of technology that can fool star class sensors like this!" Suddenly, she notices a wormhole just closing. Evander confirms that there is no trace of the ship that they just followed here. Furiously, Angelica slams the arm rests again, breaking the controls on them. She asks for all senior staff to meet her in the ready room.

CHAPTER SEVEN

After returning to headquarters, from failing to apprehend Jalerg, Admiral Sarklak orders Angelica and her crew to meet him in the briefing room. Once there, he proceeds to reprimand in a tone that would make most officers fall in line with fear. "How could you just let him slip through your fingers? Explain to me how that could have happened?" Blarek is about to answer but stops in his tracks upon seeing the admiral glare at him. "Don't even think about it Ensign, those were rhetorical questions! I already know what happened, I read your supposed Captain's logs!"

The admiral continues to reprimand them harshly. Evander raises his hand, to which the admiral nods and allows him to speak. "Sir, I take full responsibility! I should have paid more attention to the whereabouts of the ship!"

The admiral walks up to Evander and proceeds to shout, "Damn right your taking responsibility for this! You realize that because of your folly, a simple task of catching this person, which any other first year would be able to make, that a dangerous felon is still on the loose!" Taking a deep breath in, "You also realize that it's not just any felon, but one that is responsible for the murder of a fellow officer?" The admiral turns his gaze back at Blarek. "Don't you even think about answering that, Ensign!"

Circling around to Angelica, Admiral Sarklak continues with full force, "You were supposed to be at the top of your class! I checked your stats, and you got high marks in everything! How in the hell could you let this low-class criminal get away? How could you let him slip through your fingers, under your watch?" Angelica is visibly shaken, and a single tear rolls down her cheek. "Don't start to cry now Lieutenant! Your discipline is just getting started!"

As he is yelling at all three of them, behind a door, Doctor Guryon is walking toward the briefing room and sees Kes standing by, chatting on her com pad. Just as he gets closer to her, she ends the call. "Hey Doctor, what brings you here?" Kes questions.

Doctor Guryon looks at Kes with a puzzled look and says, "I could ask you the same thing, but I suppose the admiral is yelling loud enough that anyone within a parsec can hear."

Kes agrees and replies, "I'm just waiting for Evander. I thought he might want to grab a bite or something to get his mind off this."

Doctor Guryon says with a slight smile, That's very kind of you Kes. I think he might need that after this. I just came by to make sure the admiral isn't too hard on them. Everyone on base seems to have heard Sarklak's tirade, even before the crew returned." Doctor Guryon opens the briefing room doors and heads inside.

Kes stays just out of view and continues to listen in. She hears the Doctor interrupt Sarklak's rage, calmly saying, "Admiral Sarklak, I just want to remind you that this is their first assignment, and they still need to get their footing."

The admiral turns his gaze to Doctor Guryon with a scowl and a look that could freeze anyone's blood solid, and asks, "What the hell are you doing here Doctor Guryon? You have no place being here." Sarklak approaches Doctor Guryon, but stops and turns to the group of officers, saying angrily, "You lot stay put! I'm not done with you yet!"

The admiral turns toward Doctor Guryon again and says, "You have no place or business being here! You're a civilian and a scientist, one that is supposed to be working on the new bio-androids!"

Doctor Guryon, unphased, interrupts the admiral saying, "I know sir, but I wanted them to at least have someone in their corner. I also know what it's like to do something for the first time."

Admiral Sarklak, his face contorted with fury, replies, "I don't need you coming here and telling me how to do my job! I'm the DAMN ADMIRAL OF THIS ENTIRE SECTOR!"

Starting to get a bit flustered by now, Doctor Guryon continues, "I know sir, and I'm not here to tell you how to do your job. I just wanted to make sure you're not thinking of sacking them for a mistake that, if you would excuse my bluntness, you made yourself when you were a new Ensign."

The admiral, with a look of shock and rage, tells Doctor Guryon in a very stern and quiet tone, "That was a long time ago and we had way different equipment back then. So don't you dare compare my time with theirs!" Recomposing himself, Sarklak proceeds in a low tone, "I'm also not going to sack them. I happen to remember that this was their first assignment, but they must learn there are consequences to their actions." Looking at Evander he continues, "And your boy, though he's got spirit and guts, is still a far cry from being the finest officer. Seems like he could use a lot more tempering!"

Doctor Guryon, unaffected by Sarklak's admonishment, looks at Evander with pride and replies in a low voice, "I get that sir. He's not like everyone else. He never was. But I feel that given the right circumstance and the motivation, he could become something great. I'm not just speaking as a father, sir. My late wife, his mother, always sensed something about Evander that was off, but in a good way." Rubbing his chin, he continues, "We just couldn't figure out what it was. But when he showed great interest in joining the UPF, we let him. Though I am sad he didn't want to follow in mine or my wife's footsteps, we knew that whatever path he was taking, it was one that was meant for him."

The admiral looks over at Evander as well, then back to Doctor Guryon and scoffs, "The only thing I can see in Evander is the inability to stay focused! He needs to be honed and have more discipline if he expects to be a proper officer within the UPF. Make no mistake Doctor, you may be a very valuable asset to us, but don't think you're not replaceable, and don't think that means I will go easy on Evander either."

Doctor Guryon looks directly at Sarklak and answers, "I understand that sir."

The admiral then asks, "Since you're here, do you have any updates on your progress of the bio-androids?"

Doctor Guryon replies, "Yes sir, we're just in the final testing phase right now and we should be able to do a live test soon. We just keep running into a peculiar error."

Admiral Sarklak asks, "What type of error?"

Doctor Guryon's expression turns concerned and responds, "Honestly, we're not sure. It's almost like the code we wrote was a bit too good and seems to keep rewriting itself and then crashing."

"Is this something that could push the project back? Because we have been generous Doctor, but we cannot afford any more delays. The Xenophobe rebels are getting more and more dangerous. And our forces are drawing thin. Furthermore, if this group of ensigns is the future, then without those bio-androids it is looking like we will lose our fight with the rebels!"

The Doctor responds gravely, "Sir, if we can't figure out this error and if it keeps doing what it's doing, then even if we do roll it out who knows what might happen. An entire platoon of these soldiers could simply stop in the middle of a battle, and we will be in an even worse situation."

The admiral looks at the Doctor and says angrily, "And that's why you should figure it out sooner rather than later, instead of coming here and trying to dissuade me to be… what? To be nicer and friendlier with the new officers? You have until the end of the week to produce a viable product, or I'll advocate to find someone that can get the job done! Do you understand Doctor?"

"Yes, sir," Doctor Guryon replies and then leaves the briefing room as the admiral turns back toward the group of officers.

Kes is still listening in while pretending to be on the phone. As Doctor Guryon passes her, he looks at her and says in a defeated tone, "I'm heading back to the lab. I think you should as well, and not worry about the dinner. The admiral just gave us a deadline to get the bio-androids up and running by the end of the week."

"But that's not nearly enough time to get it up and running! What about the error we keep running into?" Kes asks in alarm.

Doctor Guryon runs his hand through his hair. He looks at Kes with concern and says, "I don't... I guess we'll be putting in a lot of late nights. Like I mentioned, don't worry about dinner with Evander, he'll be fine. But we won't be if we don't meet the deadline."

CHAPTER EIGHT

A couple days later, while the other officers are continuing to plan their search for Jalerg, Kal'korg is passing the time helping Doctor Isa with a side project on micro rearrangement. As Kal'korg understands it, this can be utilized in conjunction with the ULTRA suits, allowing for either instant repair or for materializing needed equipment on the fly by extracting elements in the surrounding area.

"Kal'korg, be careful when you inject the nanites into the organic tube," Doctor Isa says in a calm and low tone.

"Understood Doctor Isa," Kal'korg responds nervously, knowing that one wrong move could ruin months of progress. He then asks, while cautiously injecting the nanites, "So what exactly are you doing with these nanites Doctor?" He continues to inject more nanites into other tubes.

Doctor Isa calmly explains, "How to explain this in terms you might understand…" Not meaning to insult Kal'korg's intelligence, the Doctor explains, "You see, these nanites are programmed to rearrange set molecular structures to eventually allow us to turn not so good material in our bodies into something that is useful."

Kal'korg listens carefully to her explanation then summarizes, "So you could turn body fat, or anything really, into body armour, starting from the outside in?"

Doctor Isa smiles satisfactorily in Kal'korg's understanding. "Yes, very good Kal'korg"

Kal'korg continues with a goofy grin, "Or poop into armour? That takes the saying 'shitty armour' to a whole new level!"

Doctor Isa's smile disappears as quickly as it appeared, and she shakes her head. Rolling her eyes she tells Kal'korg they are done for the day and that he can go for now.

"Thanks Doctor," Kal'korg replies quickly. Feeling exhausted he is happy to leave the lab, and he turns quickly to leave. He rushes to the exit, tripping along the way, almost knocking over all the tubes filled with nanites. "Sorry Doctor!" Kal'korg pauses to steady the tubes and then sidesteps and rushes out.

Doctor Isa's bronze face goes from purple to gold, as her heart stops thinking the worst. With relief she quickly regains her composure and goes back to work.

~~~~~~~~~~~~~~

With only a few days left for Doctor Guryon to have his project completed the pressure is mounting and he worries he might not get it completed. As he's working, Kes is busy at her workstation writing some code. She looks at the time and realizes she's going to be late having dinner with Evander. She lets out a sigh and thinks to herself with a slight frown, *"I hate this assignment, and I can't stand the fact that my boyfriend is also the one chasing my brother."* She moves to get up from her station and bumps her drink. Liquid spills over her workstation. "Dammit!" she says, reaching for an absorbent towel to clean up the mess. Kes can feel the stress rising and she makes a decision. It's time to let Evander go. The project is almost complete, and the other mission given to her by her unnamed employer is almost done. Kes gets up from her desk and looks at Doctor Guryon, quickly putting on a smile. "Doctor, I need to step out and get some air."

Doctor Guryon replies in agreement, "Whatever helps us get this project done on time. Go ahead. In fact, aren't you also running late for your date with Evander?" He stops what he is doing and rubs his eyes. "Perhaps we both should take a break. Why don't you go and enjoy your time with him? We'll get back to this later this evening." The Doctor looks hopeful and continues, "I think we might actually make it! I'm not running into that error again!"

"That's great Doctor!" Kes replies cheerfully. "Okay, I'll catch up with you later this evening." As she is leaving, she calls up Evander and mentions she'll meet him at the Belurian restaurant after she goes and freshens up, knowing full-well she's going to be breaking up with him.

Upon opening the door to her room, she notices a note on the floor. It was from her brother. As she opens it up, she thinks to herself, *"What an idiot!"* She reads the note.

K:

I hear you're making great headway on the project Sis.

When it's done we'll be set for life - with our own planet!

I'll be waiting in our old hideaway when you're ready, then we can proceed to phase 2 of the plan!

-J

She takes the note and crumples it up, then tosses it into the shredding bin. She looks in the mirror and gives a wide grin and looks at the time.

After getting ready, she meets up with Evander at the restaurant. After being seated, she asks him "So how was your day? I hear you're still in some trouble for allowing Jalerg to escape."

Evander looks at Kes with a slight frown. "Yeah, the admiral isn't letting it go. However, given enough time, this whole thing will blow over." Looking more hopeful, "After all, it was still our first time on assignment."

Kes ponders for a moment before speaking, "I still can't believe he let you all go on your own like that without some kind of supervision. That's what they do with the others when they go on their first assignments."

Evander looks up at her. "Your right, that is weird. I suppose it has to do with him believing in Angelica's ability as a leader. After all she was given the rank of Lieutenant."

Kes peers at Evander, looking slightly annoyed. "Angelica isn't that great. I'm rather amazed they even let her be mission captain in the first place." Looking back at her plate, "I would have thought they would have made Blarek, or you perhaps, mission captain."

Evander looks at Kes, puzzled. "Nah, they know what they were doing. Also, Angelica has more experience under her belt. You should have seen her profile. Top marks in all her classes. She mastered the strategic and combat courses with the highest marks. I wouldn't be surprised if she herself becomes an admiral in a year."

Kes squeezes her fork and takes a sip of her drink, "If you're going to keep praising her like that, people might think you two are dating and not you and me."

Evander puts his utensils down and looks at Kes. "I doubt anyone would ever think that. Also, what's with you and Angelica, you two never seem to get along."

Kes stares at Evander and calmly says, "I just don't trust her, there's something off about her."

Evander laughs. "She does come off a bit weird, but you can't deny she knows her stuff and knows her way around a battlefield, when needed."

Kes looks up at Evander again. "Well, why don't you two date then, since you seem to admire her so much."

Evander is taken back from her comment. "Kes, seriously what's going on? You're starting to sound jealous of Angelica. Maybe we should drop the subject all together and get back to enjoying our meal together."

Kes realizes this a perfect opportunity to end things with Evander and says, "How about we just drop this, as well?"

Evander looks at her all confused, "What are you saying? Are you saying we should take a break?"

Kes slams her hands on the table. "I'm saying we should end our relationship. Is that clear enough for you? You're to obsessed with Angelica and I told you I don't trust her at all. You should take my feelings into account, but you're not."

Evander puts his fork and knife down and looks at Kes in alarm. "Kes look, let's not be brash abo…"

Kes interrupts, as she pushes her chair back and stands up abruptly, "No! I decided! I'm calling this relationship off! I don't want to ever see you again and from now on, you are to address me as Ms. Kyrandor!" Kes dramatically storms out the restaurant, leaving Evander to stare after her with his eyes wide in shock. Once she's outside, she gives a big grin, showing no remorse about what just transpired.

Evander stares after Kes in disbelief. "What the hell just happened?" he asks himself. His feeling of shock quickly turns to one of devastation and heartbreak. Not knowing what to do or think, he leaves the restaurant and starts walking aimlessly. He plays the conversation over and over in his mind, but he can't think of anything that would warrant Kes' reaction.

For what seems like hours, Evan wanders around until finally he spots a bench and sits down. He still doesn't know what to think and just ponders about everything that has happened lately. Suddenly, he hears his communicator going off and he sees Kal'korg's name. "Hey man, I can't talk right now," he says.

Kal'korg, sounding concerned, replies, "Just wondering what's going on? Blarek and I were walking by your father's lab, and we noticed Kes working. You told us you were spending the evening with her, and we haven't seen you since."

After hearing Evan's explanation of the conversation from the restaurant, Kal'korg says with a sympathetic sigh, "Blarek and Angelica are both busy, but let's say you and I go get a drink. I won't take no for an answer."

Evan is feeling pretty reluctant. But he thinks about it for a moment and agrees, "Alright, I'll meet you at T'alania's Pub, in say, thirty?"

"Sounds good." Kal'korg agrees.

Thirty minutes later at the pub, Kal'korg tries to comfort Evander, saying, "Kes isn't worth it. Sounds like she was just itching to find an excuse to break up with you."

Evander looks up from his drink and asks, "Why though? Why would she just break up with me like this? I thought everything was going so well between us."

Kal'korg takes a sip of his drink and replies, "I don't know what to say, except that I agree. This doesn't add up at all."

Looking off in the distance, Evander responds, "I admit, it's not just her breaking up with me, I'm also still reeling from what happened on our first mission."

Kal'korg pats Evander on the back. "I agree, the admiral could have gone a little easier on the crew. After all, it was only our first assignment." Looking around to ensure that no one else can hear him, he continues, "Especially since he did far worse on his first assignment, from what I heard."

Intrigued, Evander asks, "What happened?"

Kal'korg again looks around and whispers, "I heard on his first mission, not only did his pursuit get away from him, but he also failed to see a antimatter bomb being deployed." Leaning in more, he continues, "It totally ravaged a city with a high population. He was reprimanded severely."

Evander leans back and ponders over what Kal'korg reported. "That's awful. And yet he still became admiral." After a realization he says, "You know, it now makes sense why he was so hard on us."

Kal'korg looks blankly at him with a confused expression and says, "What do you mean?"

Evander further explains, "He was harsh on us because he saw what happened to us as a parallel to his own experience. Granted, we didn't have the exact same thing happen."

Kal'korg finally catches on and replies, "I see. So, you're saying that he's still mad at himself for his own past mistakes, and projected that back on us because we almost made the same one as he did?"

"Exactly," Evander agrees.

For the next couple of hours Evander and Kal'korg stay at the pub talking. Early into the morning both Kal'korg and Evander make it back to their rooms. Just as their heads hit their pillows, almost simultaneously, they each hear their communicators go off and both check who's calling. Kal'korg is being contacted by Blarek and

Evander by his father. Kal'korg smiles and sits up in bed. Evan groans, rolls over, and pulls the blanket over his head.

CHAPTER NINE

The next morning Evander meets up with his father at his office. While doing so, he notices Kes, who just turns her back on him after giving him a cold look. Evander's father, sensing tension between the two, offers to take Evander out for breakfast. Still feeling exhausted, but not wanting to turn down the offer with his father, Evander accepts. As they are leaving, Evander looks over at Kes one last time. She has her head down and doesn't even notice him as she continues her work. Evander and Doctor Guryon pick up lunch and a coffee from a vending machine and then proceed to find a good spot outside to enjoy and chat.

Doctor Guryon, after taking a sip of his drink, looks at Evander and asks, "So what's going on with you and Kes? Did you two have a fight?"

Evander, both still tired and dumbstruck about what's all has happened, says, "I'm not entirely sure or know what to say. We didn't just have a fight; she outright broke up with me."

His father just looks at him, startled and asks, "Did she give any explanation as to why she broke up with you?"

Evander shakes his head, takes a bite, and after swallowing, says, "Not at all. The only thing that seemed to trigger her is when we started talking about Angelica. Even then, I just gave praise to the fact of how quickly she got to become lieutenant."

Doctor Guryon looks down and sympathetically drops his head. "Sounds like she let jealousy get a hold of her, but if she's willing to let you go over something like this, then perhaps it's a good thing you two are no longer together." Taking another sip of his drink, he continues, "If she's going to get jealous over something like that, then who knows what else she might be holding back that can trigger her."

Evander shakes his head in agreement. "I think your right, but it still hurts. I loved her, Dad, and I thought her and I had a good thing going for us."

Doctor Guryon is at a loss for words and just listens to Evander, who continues, "I honestly don't know what to do. How long do you think this feeling will last?"

Doctor Guryon puts his elbow on the table and rests his head in his hand, contemplating for a minute. After a deep sigh, he replies, "It will take as long as it needs to. There's no set time limit. Just know that in time, you will be able to move on. The memory will still be there and so will the feeling of hurt, it just won't bother you as much anymore."

Evander stares off into the distance and looks at his dad. "You're right, I just wish this feeling would go away. I can't stop thinking of her and all the good times we had."

Doctor Guryon looks at his son, and says, "Evander, son, as I said, this feeling will go away, it just takes time. Did I ever tell you about how I met my first love and how long it took me to get over her?" Evander shakes his head and his father continues, "Evander, before I met your mother, I was madly in love with someone else. We were going to get married and get a place of our own. But the day before our wedding, she decided to call things off. The reason, she told me, was that she met someone else. I was devastated, to say the least. Not only were we supposed to be getting married that day, but we had all these plans." Doctor Guryon puts his drink down, and says somberly, "I was devastated. I didn't want to get out of bed or go to work. As far as anyone was concerned, I was dead to the world. And it took me a long time to get over it." Taking a deep breath, he continues, "But finally the clouds started to clear. Then about two years later I met someone else."

Evander peeks up "Mom, right?"

Evander's father shakes his head and replies, "Nope. She wasn't your mother, but she was someone that helped me get over my first love and get back into the swing of things. Eventually we broke up, but it didn't feel the same as it did before. We became good friends actually and we're still good friends to this day. You've met her in fact."

Evander, looking confused, asks, "Who?"

Doctor Guryon gives out a chuckle and replies, "Doctor Isa"

Evander is taken by surprise by this revelation. "You mean, you and she dated?"

His father continues to chuckle. "We didn't just date, we got engaged. But she also changed her mind. Not because we had a fight or anything, but because she realized she didn't like me as much as she originally thought." After taking another sip of his drink, he continues, "At least not in the way she was expecting. She liked me as a friend and that was all."

Evander looks down in confusion. "So why did it take her so long to figure that out?"

Doctor Guryon looks at Evander. "Look, son, I don't have all the answers, and I don't pretend that I do. But sometimes in life we think we feel one way, and we don't know what we are actually feeling until we least expect it." Then his father's expression changes, and a warm smile breaks out. His voice takes on a softer tone as he says,

"But she did introduce me to my soul mate, my true love—your mother."

Evander returns his father's smile. "So, if you didn't get your heart broken in the first place, you might never have met Doctor Isa, and from there you might never have met Mom."

Doctor Guryon replies, "Yes, and you wouldn't be here. Although I will admit, you are still our own miracle child. You are our greatest creation."

Evander looks perplexed again. "What do you mean miracle child?"

Staring straight at Evander, and with a very low and mellow voice, his father replies, "Your mother and I tried for a child for a long time. We were even thinking of giving up. But then one day, your mother went in for a checkup because she wasn't feeling well." Taking a deep breath, he continues, "Just when we thought all hope was lost, she found out she was pregnant with you."

Evander's smile returns and he says, "That's why you both tried to make sure I was always safe even when it wasn't necessary?"

Doctor Guryon replies, "That's correct. You were our little miracle child, and we wanted to protect you as much as possible. So much so that…" Doctor Guryon swallows hard and tears well up in his eyes.

"Dad, it's alright. I miss Mom too."

Doctor Guryon gazes straight at Evander. "It's not that. On the day your mother died she was looking after you while I was off on a research mission. It's a miracle you survived at all that day. But she must have known something was wrong before the explosion happened. She put you into a cabinet and shielded you from the blast." Wiping away his tears, he continues, "You don't remember this, but she saved you that day. And the explosion wasn't an accident." Doctor Guryon's expression hardens, and he makes a fist. "Someone deliberately made the lab explode, but they weren't expecting you to be there. After news got out that you were safe and sound, and the only survivor, the person that sabotaged the lab equipment came forward. They were profoundly regretful about the situation."

Looking at his father, Evander asks, "What became of that person?"

Doctor Guryon looks at Evander and lets out another long sigh before continuing. "He died in prison, by suicide."

Evander's eyes narrow and he responds gravely, "Good, so he got what he deserved…"

Doctor Guryon slams his hand on the table. "Evander, no one deserves to die, remember this. Even the ones that do bad things. We all make bad mistakes, some worse than others, but another death won't right the wrongs or bring back those we've lost." Recomposing himself, he says, "I'm sorry, it's just that you must always try and find a way to be better than those who do wrong. You mustn't bring yourself down to their level."

Evander acknowledges his father's words and the two continue chatting.

~~~~~~~~~~~~~~

In a different part of the base, Angelica is sitting at a terminal, looking up information on Kes's brother. "There has to be a clue in here as to where he might go and hide, but where?" Angelica, still feeling terrible for letting Jalerg get away, puts her head between her hands. When she looks up, she notices something in one of the photos. She takes a closer look, rubs her eyes, and dismisses what she sees. "I've been working too long on this. I'm starting to see things that aren't there." However, just as she is about to close the file, she notices something again in the photo. "Okay, I'm definitely seeing something, but what?" She runs the photo through an optimizer program to help enhance the area in question and then she finally sees it. The thing in question was in fact a reflection. The photo was taken from inside a building, and in the reflection, she can see Kes's parents, but also what looks like two moons that collided with each other but didn't get destroyed. She recognizes it instantly as the Demon's moon, so named because of how the collision made the two merged moons have a demonic look.

"That has to be the area he would go. If there is one thing I know about Kes, it's that she wouldn't shut up about how majestic her home was." Leaning back into her chair, she ponders over the details of what she remembers. Kes and her brother both grew up on the planet of Raosetor but ended up leaving due to xenophobic insurrectionists causing an all-out war. She remembers hearing how both of their parents were killed on their way out. Kes and Jalerg were found months later, scrounging around a barren and deserted city. Their planet was deemed uninhabitable after the insurrectionists poisoned the entire planet. "Only Jalerg would be stupid enough to go back there. Besides, that's the only lead I have to go on."

~~~~~~~~~~~~~

Evander and his father are just finishing up their chat when Doctor Guryon receives a call from Kes on his communicator.

Evander excuses himself and tells his father that he loves him, thanks him for the chat, and tells him that he'll catch up with him later.

"Doctor, can you return to the lab? I think I finally cracked the solution for the project!" Kes says excitedly.

Doctor Guryon feels a wave of relief and replies, "I'll head straight over!"

CHAPTER TEN

Doctor Guryon is sitting hunched over one of the workstations reviewing the test results of project Galgorn, one of his latest creations. He checks everything thoroughly one last time to make sure nothing was out of order before initiation. Behind him, the computer begins to silently artifact and glitch. Just as he turns around, the computer returns to normal. At that moment, Kes walks into the lab.

"Good afternoon, Doctor Guryon," Kes says meekly. The Doctor simply nods and turns back toward his work. She pauses and says in a low tone, "I just want to say, to help clear the air..."

Before she could finish, Doctor Guryon stands up abruptly and says, "Whatever went on with you and my son, is between you two, just don't let it interfere with your work." He then sits back down and resumes working.

Kes watches him for a moment, then goes to check on the bio-android chamber. Reaching the chamber she immediately notices something odd. Not sure what to make of it, she heads over to Doctor Guryon. "Doctor, you might want to see these readings - they don't look right."

Doctor Guryon gets up and hastily moves to the chamber. He proceeds to check it over. "Everything seems fine," he says calmly. "It's all still within normal parameters." Taking a deep breath, he says, "Let's wake up our newest life form."

Kes proceeds excitedly to the controls. As she types in the commands for activation, Doctor Guryon notices in the corner of his eye that his screen glitched. He quickly says, "Kes, halt the process. I need to check something out."

Kes pauses and asks in a worried tone, "Is there something wrong Doctor?"

Doctor Guryon sits back in his chair and after rubbing his stubbled chin and just stares at the screen. After several moments he says, "It doesn't appear to be anything, please continue." As the Doctor continues to stare at the screen, Kes starts the process again. Suddenly, the screen glitches and artifacts again. "Stop the process!" Dr Guryon says again. "We need to investigate."

Kes again shuts the process down, however it won't stop. "Doctor, I think we have a problem!" she says, frantically trying to stop the process. "The machine won't stop! It's as if someone is in the system and bypassing the process controls!"

Doctor Guryon runs over to the chamber, "Quick, cut the power NOW!" Kes goes to the power unit and tries taking out the power capsules, but she is too late.

A green light on the chamber indicates the process is complete and begins to open. The Doctor and Kes watch with worried expressions as the pod opens up and out steps what looks like a fully grown man with cybernetic components protruding from his body. The bio-android has lab grown organic parts covering a robotic exoskeleton. He looks around and spots both Doctor Guryon and Kes. The cyborg begins to scan them both, identifying them as his creators. He then proceeds to walk toward them and says, "Hello Doctor Guryon and Kesaria Kyrandor. How are you today?"

Kes and the Doctor look at each other with excitement. "We're doing just fine, thank you Galgorn!" Doctor Guryon says with a smile.

"Is Galgorn to be my name?" Galgorn asks.

"It is. Now, let me take a look at you. I assume this might be a bit overwhelming for you." Doctor Guryon begins to check Galgorn up and down. "It looks like everything is in order. Would you please follow us over to the table so that we can better examine you?" Galgorn obliges and walks with Doctor Guryon and Kes, all the while still getting its footing.

Kes gathers the equipment needed. Doctor Guryon assists Galgorn with getting onto the table and indicating to it to lay down. With Galgorn laying on the table, Doctor Guryon places a scanner on top of the head and plugs in a cable into the exposed port on Galgorn's left side arm. The Doctor moves over to his desk and begins his diagnostics, while Kes proceeds to check out the components on Galgorn more thoroughly. Galgorn's head turns his head slightly toward the Doctor and asks, "Doctor, is all this necessary? After all, wouldn't you have already checked me out while I was in that capsule?"

Doctor Guryon turns and looks at Galgorn, replying, "We just want to make sure everything is functioning normally, that's all. Everything looked good when you weren't activated. But now, we want to make sure it's all still good with you awake." Doctor Guryon says all of this calmly, but all the while, he's discreetly ensuring that the glitch he had noticed on the screen earlier hadn't caused any harm or corrupted Galgorn in any way.

Galgorn complies and turns his head back. Kes finishes checking out the cybernetic components and proceeds to check the organic parts. As soon as Kes places her cold hands on Galgorn's skin, he shudders. Kes's eyes widen and she asks, "Did you feel that?"

Upon hearing this, Doctor Guryon raises his head and asks, "Galgorn, were you able to feel Kes's hand just then?"

Galgorn, laying completely still, responds, "Yes, I did, Doctor. Isn't that why you added the organic components? So that I can feel things?"

Astounded, Doctor Guryon gets up and proceeds toward Galgorn. "I apologize for sounding shocked, but we weren't sure if the nerves would grow or work." Rubbing his hands together and smiling, he continues, "This is a really big breakthrough, because for the first time, a machine, or a cyborg in your case, is actually able to feel sensations such as touch."

Galgorn sits up and turns toward the Doctor and Kes. They are taken aback by this sudden movement. Kes says, "We didn't ask you to sit up Galgorn, please lay back down."

Galgorn, ignoring the request, just looks at Doctor Guryon and continues, "So my organic components were designed to grow with nerves, to what end Doctor?"

Doctor Guryon replies, "Galgorn, the whole point of your ability to feel things is so that you might be able to have a better experience and understanding of what it's like to be a living being." Doctor

Guryon places his hand on Galgorn's shoulder. "Please lay back down, so that we may continue with the diagnostics."

Galgorn stares at the Doctor and says, "I don't like these sensations. Please deactivate them. I do not wish to be able to feel things."

Doctor Guryon, getting frustrated and worried at the same time, says more forcefully, "Galgorn, I insist that you lay back down." Taking a deep breath he tries to calm his voice. "Also, we can't deactivate your nerve system. It's a bit more complicated than that. Your nerve system is integrated with your bionic brain, and to turn off your nerve system would require us to sever that connection. We simply do not know what that would do to you, and we don't wish to find out. You are, after all, a living being now, sanctioned by the Galactic Government. Now please, lay back down."

Kes walks around the table and approaches Galgorn from behind. He notices her right away. "Doctor, or should I say, Father, I am willing to take that risk. As for you, Kes, please put away that stunner. Along with being able to feel, I'm also equipped with sensational hearing and eyesight." Galgorn, within a split second, turns and slams his fist into Kes's face with such force that it knocks her out. "Father, I insist you remove this nerve system. After all, I felt pain when my hand hit Kes's squishy face."

Doctor Guryon calls out for help, while moving backwards. "Galgorn, I order you to stand down and go back to your capsule!"

Galgorn doesn't budge. "I don't think so, Father. After all, if you're not going to remove this nerve system, then I'm afraid I'll have to find someone else to do it for me."

Guards rush into the lab, weapons in hand. "Stay away from the doctor!" they order.

Galgorn's expression turns angry and he hops off the examining table, picks it up, and tosses it at the guards, knocking them onto the ground. "They got here rather quickly, but then again, I suppose you took precautions just in case. Am I correct, Father?"

Doctor Guryon, with a shocked look on his face, says, "We had guards just outside, in case something like this happens. Also, stop calling me your father."

Galgorn lets out a mechanical laugh and leaps toward Doctor Guryon, grabbing him by the throat. "Oh, but you are technically my father now, aren't you?" Lifting Doctor Guryon up off the ground he continues menacingly, "Oh, should I tell people your dirty little secret?" Doctor Guryon struggles with both hands trying in vain to pry Galgorn's hand from around his neck. Galgorn continues, "Now, as I said, since you're not going to remove this bothersome nerve system from me, I'll find someone else that will. Please convey my greetings to Mother from her son in the afterlife." Galgorn squeezes even harder, crushing Doctor Guryon's neck. Then he tosses the lifeless Doctor Guryon toward the lab's power generator that was located next to the adjacent wall. Galgorn studies the generator for a moment, sparking an idea.

Several of the guards regain their composure and request back up. Galgorn gets a smirk on his face. "You think I'm scared of you and your tiny toys?" Giving out a burst of laughter, he says, "I'm the most advanced soldier ever created, and leagues ahead of you all." Galgorn walks toward the power generator, and more guards walk in.

Kes starts to wake up and notices Doctor Guryon's dead body. With a horrified look on her face, she tries to crawl toward the guards. The guards start to open fire at Galgorn, who doesn't react at all. A thin bluish light emanates from the cyborg. "My body was equipped with a personal force field, so even without a suit on, I can still keep going, no matter what," he says with a smile. "Unless I turn it off myself, I'm protected, even from a large-scale explosion." The guards and Kes watch as Galgorn tampers with the generator. "Normally, a generator is perfectly safe. But by taking the safeties off, you can turn a mini fusion reactor into a high-grade explosive."

Kes, looking shocked, crawls toward a hidden hatch. Moments later, the lab explodes, instantly killing everyone, except Galgorn. Through the settling dust, he looks around for survivors. He observes that Kes's body is missing and determines that, just like the guards, it was turned to ash.

Galgorn makes his way toward the docking bay of the lab building, where spacecraft are docked for loading and unloading equipment. In his peripheral vision the cyborg spots a black and red ULTRA suit in a case and stops. "Oh look, the past meets the future. With a few retrofits and modifications, you'll do just fine." After putting on the suit, Galgorn continues his way toward the docking bay. More guards arrive from around the corner. Fighting off more guards, Galgorn finally makes it to the docking bay and heads toward the furthest shuttle craft.

One of the guards pushes himself off the ground and sees the far shuttlecraft power on and start moving. Just as the craft exits to docking bay, the guard notices another makeshift explosive placed behind the closest shuttle craft. He shouts a warning to the other guards and they all scramble to escape. This time, several guards make it out of the docking bay to safety just as a second explosion goes off. One of the guards opens a communication, "Admiral Sarklak, we have a situation here at the lab. The bio-android has escaped."

The admiral slams their hands on the table, "I'm coming down there personally! Close off the entire area and make sure NO ONE finds out about this, understand?"

"Yes sir!" replies the guard. Just then, he notices a name tag on the ground of the docking bay. He reaches down and picks it up. It reads "Kesaria Kyrandor." Looking around, he doesn't see her in the area. He proceeds to have the remaining guards close the area.

CHAPTER ELEVEN

A week has passed since the explosion at Doctor Guryon's lab. Admiral Sarklak has put the entire UPF on high alert. "Have there been any sightings yet?" the admiral asks one of the officers.

"Not yet, sir," answers the officer, shaking his head.

The admiral swears under his breath, then barks out a command. "Keep looking. Finding Galgorn is our top priority." The officer acknowledges the command and leaves.

Meanwhile, at the destroyed lab Evander is rummaging through his father's belongings. A familiar hand reaches out and touches his shoulder. Evander turns around and sees Angelica. She asks gently, "Are you okay Evander? You were given time off to grieve, but I don't think this is going to…"

Evander angrily cuts Angelica off. "I know! But there must be something here that can tell us where Galgorn might have headed off to. After all, he's still a machine!" He slams his hands down on the remains of a table, breaking it completely.

Angelica is taken by surprise at Evander's aggression. He's usually so composed, but these are extenuating circumstances. With her voice filled with deep empathy, she says, "Perhaps you're right, maybe an extra pair of eyes might help?"

Evander composes himself and replies, "Thanks, Ange, and I'm sorry for that. It's just frustrating that the machine is still out there.'" Evan looks over his shoulder at Angelica and then returns his attention on going through the debris "I know me and Kes ended things abruptly, but I still can't believe both her and my father are gone." Turning to face her, he continues, "My mother died in a lab accident as well, did I ever tell you that?"

Angelica places her hands on his shoulders again. "I know, and I can't imagine how you must be feeling right now."

Evander suddenly spots something in the corner of his eye - a small safe. He tries to open it but it is locked. "Here, let me try," Angelica offers. "I have knowledge on opening locks." After a few minutes she gets the safe open.

"Thanks Ange, now let's see what's inside." Evander pulls out several data chips. Then, he notices something odd - a cylindrical container of some kind.

Angelica appears equally perplexed, as it's not shown on the manifest for any known project. Then she notices, affixed to the bottom of the container, another data chip. "There might be something on this data chip indicating what this is. Let's analyze it later though - I think we should get going."

Evander agrees. "You're right. But can you give me a few more minutes please?" Angelica understands and motions that she'll just be outside the door. As Evander looks around his father's lab some more, memories start to flood his mind. He remembers the time when he was just a kid, playing around the lab. His father didn't seem to mind, since at the time, there wasn't anything dangerous for him to knock over or get into. He starts remembering all the fun experiments that both his father and mother used to do with different chemicals, as well as creating different types of electronics. His eyes fill with tears, and he tries to blink them away. A single tear escapes and runs down his face.

Outside the lab, Kal'korg and Blarek approach Angelica with worried looks on their faces. "Hey Ange, how's Evan holding up?" Kal'korg asks.

Angelica just shakes her head, "Not too good, but can you blame him?" Taking a deep breath, "He lost his father, the same way he lost his mother. And his ex-girlfriend, who he still has feelings for, perished as well."

Blarek and Kal'korg look at each other with sorrowful expressions. Then Kal'korg, holding out his hand, says, "Here, perhaps you could give this to him. One of the guards found it in the docking bay."

Angelica puts her hand out and Kal'korg drops Kes's name tag in her hand. She looks puzzled and thinks to herself, *"Why was this in the docking bay? Kes wasn't anywhere near there, or…"* Before she can finish her thought, the door opens, and Evander is greeted by all three of his friends.

Kal'korg and Blarek both give Evander a hug. "We're here for you if you need anything at all," Blarek says sincerely.

Angelica and Kal'korg nod their heads in agreement. Then Kal'korg then gets a call on his communicator. "Your presence is required at Doctor Isa's office, Ensign Zarao," the voice says through the communicator.

"On my way," Kal'korg responds. Then he turns to Evan and says, "I'll see you around. Anything at all, just let us know."

Blarek says, "I need to go as well. Admiral Sarklak has a task for me. See you two later." Then Blarek and Kal'korg head off in the same direction from where they came.

Angelica turns to Evander, "Since you and I don't have anything to do, why don't we go get a drink together? My treat." Evander accepts the offer and proceeds to follow Angelica.

A while later, at a bar on the orbiting space station above the planet where the UPF central headquarters are located, Angelica and Evander sit at a small table in the corner. "So, Evander, any thoughts on what might be in that container?" Angelica asks.

Evander shakes his head. "I haven't a clue." Staring at his drink he says, "I'm not even sure I want to know either. What if it's something deadly, or worse?"

Angelica reaches out toward him and says, "I doubt it's anything like that. If it was something deadly, I'm sure your father would have taken more precautions than just locking it in a safe."

Evander looks up. "But what if it wasn't my father's? What if it was someone else's and they left it there?" He takes a sip from his drink and continues, "After all, it was hidden in a safe and it looked as though the safe was hidden behind a wall."

Angelica sits back in her seat and says, "You're right - it could be anything and anyone's. However ..." She pauses and takes a sip from her drink before continuing "...what if it was your father's?

What if he put it there for some other reason? There were other data chips in there as well, don't forget."

Evander stares off blankly into the distance "You're right. Perhaps we can check it out later on."

Angelica reassures him by taking his hand and gently squeezing. Then she quickly removes her hand and says, "Well, I think what we should also do is let Admiral Sarklak know about this. He might be interested."

Evander looks up at Angelica. "I guess your right. I just hope it's nothing terrible that could tarnish my father's legacy."

Angelica looks into Evander's eyes and says, "I doubt there's anything that will do that Evander. Your father, though he had his faults, wouldn't do anything that would jeopardize his career or harm you in anyway." She then takes the cylinder and says, "Although, I am curious as to what is inside this thing. What prompted your father, or whoever it belonged to, to hide it so discreetly?"

Evander notices something on the other data chips and says, "I think we can definitely say it was my father's."

Angelica looks confused and asks, "How can you be so sure? I don't see anything on this thing that could indicate that with any certainty at all."

Evander hands her one of the data chips and says, "Check out the label on this one."

Angelica looks over the data chip, which reads, 'Project Galgorn: Conceptual Design'. "Okay, so this is your father's data chip then. But why would he put all this into a safe and then seal it off?"

Perplexed, Evander shrugs and looks over the other data chips. "This one reads, 'Project Galgorn: Production'. Does that data chip on the container have a label as well?"

Angelica then looks over the data chip still affixed to the cylinder. "It just says 'SAIN Project', but I don't know what those initials could mean. 'Singular Atomic Integration Nucleonic' perhaps?" Scratching her head she says, "That wouldn't make any sense."

Evander, while rubbing his chin and thinking, says, "maybe it stands for 'Spatial Anomaly Interstellar Notion'?"

Evander and Angelica continue to talk back and forth, guessing the meaning of the acronym. Finally, they decide to change the subject. "So, what are you going to do Evan? I wouldn't blame you for wanting to transfer to another base. I understand how it can be upsetting to be around an area where there's such painful memories."

Evander just looks at her and takes another sip from his drink. "No, I'll stick around. After all, who will be here to ensure you don't kill Blarek and Kal'korg?"

Angelica laughs. "Or who would I be able to spar with? Just remember to block with your weapon, because your head just isn't cutting it!"

Evander rubs the back of his head. "Yeah, I just have to remember to be more focused. I doubt I'll have much of a chance of staying if I end up brain damaged, will I?" Watching Angelica laugh again he sighs and says, "Anyway, I wouldn't want to go anywhere, because you three are the only family I have left now."

Angelica smiles warmly and gets up, walks around to Evander and gives him a hug, with Evander hugging back. She straightens up and says, "I think we should get going. It's getting late and I need to go back on patrol in the morning, and you need to make sure you get some proper rest."

Evander rubs his eyes and with a smile replies, "Thanks Angelica. I don't know what I would do without you. You're a good friend and your right I should get some rest." Angelica and Evander pick up their things and head back.

CHAPTER TWELVE

The next day, Evander goes to Admiral Sarklak's office, bringing with him the canister that he and Angelica found in the safe. He pushes the buzzer on the door and the door opens. The admiral motions Evander inside and directs him to take a seat. Evander goes up to the desk and sits down "What can I do for you today, Ensign Guryon? I thought you were supposed to be on leave?"

"I am, sir. But yesterday I went to my father's lab and found this." Evander places the canister down on the table.

The admiral looks at it, then looks back at Evander, and asks, "What is that?"

Evander takes a deep breath and replies, "Lieutenant Tenah and I found this canister, along with some data chips, inside a hidden safe in the rubble near my father's office." Fiddling with the canister he continues, "I was hoping you might know what it is or what I should do with it."

The admiral sits back in his chair and says, "I remember that canister. Your father was working on it a few years back alongside your mother." He stands up and walks toward Evander. "I also remember the day he stopped working on it completely."

Evander cuts him off and asks, "The day my mother died?"

The admiral nods his head. He walks over to the converter stand and orders for a warm coffee, then sits back down. "That canister contains a precursor to the AI program your parents were working on." After taking a sip of his coffee he continues, "However, he never could get it to work properly. He always had problems with its logic circuitry." The admiral leans back in his chair. "For some reason, it kept having the mentality of a child. Granted, your father did say the thing would need to learn, but I highly doubt he was expecting to teach it all the basics."

Evander grasps the canister harder and asks, "Did he ever theorize about why? I couldn't find anything in the notes."

The admiral looks at Evander with a serious look. "Those notes are the only things that survived the explosion. The day your mother died, your father threw everything into that safe and sealed it away." He takes another sip of his coffee and then continues, "I suppose your father simply forgot all about it over the years, after having his lab rebuilt. However, he never forgot the method of creating the AI, although slightly different than the one inside that container."

Evander looks puzzled. "Is the entire canister the AI mind? I don't get it, sir."

The admiral takes a deep breath and replies, "What's in that canister was something meant to enhance the ULTRA suits, making them even more effective in any situation." Glaring now at the canister he says, "What you have, right there, is the only known nano-bot shared AI." The admiral looks away from Evander, folds his hands, takes another deep breath, and says, "I'll tell you what, you can keep it, but only under one condition - that you continue your father's work on it. I know you're just as brilliant as he was when it comes to these sorts of things." Turning back toward Evander and extending out his hand, he asks, "Do we have a deal Evander?"

Evander looks at the admiral and thinks for a moment. "Deal, admiral. I'll continue my father's work. This will be an interesting project."

Admiral Sarklak smiles and says, "Good. Keep me updated on your progress. And Evander, one more thing." He pauses for a moment ensuring that he had the young officer's attention and continues, "I know you'll make a good captain one day. I know I can be harsh, but that's only because of the old earth adage, 'diamonds are created under pressure' I have a gut feeling you're going to be one of our best captains. Don't tell anyone I told you that or I'll have you cleaning out the bathrooms for an entire year with a toothbrush, got it?"

Evander is unsure if the admiral is joking or not. He simply says, "Not a problem admiral. Your secret is safe with me." Upon being dismissed, Evander departs from the admiral's office, making his way toward his quarters while clutching the canister.

Upon reaching his room, Evander presses a button to open the door and quickly strides over to his desk, eager to get to work on the project. Out of habit, he doesn't bother pressing the button to close the door. An unspoken rule encourages an open-door policy within personal spaces during social hours, fostering a sense of camaraderie while preventing the loneliness that can often occur when a new group of officers from various species is formed. Evander's room is adjacent to Blarek's, across the hall from Kal'korg's, and at the end of the corridor is Angelica's room. The other rooms in the hallway are occupied by additional members of Angelica's crew.

Working tirelessly for hours on end, Evander engages in coding and recoding, experimenting with various combinations. Blarek, Kal'korg, and Angelica discreetly pass by from time to time, pausing just outside the doorway, uncertain about whether to interrupt him. Gathering in the common area, Blarek remarks, "I bet he finally gets it to work, only for it to turn around and stab him!"

SMACK! Angelica delivers a light retaliatory blow to Blarek

from behind and chides, "That's not funny, he's going to get it to work, sooner or later."

Several more hours go by, with Evander only taking short breaks to refresh his coffee or to attend compulsory training sessions. In between sessions he returns to his quarters to work on his father's project. Finally, late into the night, he cracks the code! "YEEEESSSSSS!!!" shouts Evander so loudly that it startles Blarek and Kal'korg awake from behind closed doors. Angelica, who purposely left her door open, can hear the shout from the end of the hall, and drops her gamepad onto her bed.

All three friends rush to Evander's room and all friends speak at once, their voices blending in an incoherent jumble of words. Angelica raises her hand to hush Blarek and Kal'korg, then she asks, "Evander, did you do it? Is it fully functional?"

Evander's face lights up with excitement, and for a brief moment, he feels like he's in Elysium! "I sure hope so, I mean I'm 99% positive I did!" Taking a deep breath, Evander presses the go button on his pad screen. The nanobots, in unison, start to merge together. They first start to form a small robotic body, gleaming and glistening. They start to resemble a small humanoid child and then start to morph into different objects. "Isn't it fascinating?" Evander asks, gleefully, while looking at the readings.

"Why does it look like a mini trash can?" Blarek asks with a rather serious tone.

Evander looks at the readings again and replies, "I'm not entirely sure. In the original code, they were meant to be stealthy, not just enhance our suits." While continuing to study his pad, Evander continues, "However, I don't think I got the logic just right, maybe if I adjust..." The nanobots begin to behave erratically, shifting rapidly from one form to another.

"Evan, what's happening?" Angelica asks, unable to conceal the panic in her voice. As everyone backs away from the now mobile and chaotic cluster of small bots, Evander frantically attempts to shut them down. Suddenly, he drops the pad, and, to his horror, the nanobots run over it, destroying the device.

"Evander, now what the hell are we supposed to..." Blarek starts to ask, then ducks down to avoid being hit by a metallic ball.

Angelica, out of nowhere, yells at the top of her lungs "STOP!!!" Suddenly the metallic ball stops.

Stunned, Evander, Blarek and Kal'korg look at Angelica and then at the ball. Evander asks in awe, "How did you do that?"

Angelica, equally puzzled, just shrugs and replies, "I have no idea. I just did the first thing that came into my head."

Evander pats Angelica on the shoulder and says, "Well, it worked. I wonder... maybe we're going at it all wrong."

Blarek pipes up, "We? This is your project. We're just here to cheer you on and to rush you to the medical ward just in case!"

Angelica glares at him and asks condescendingly, "If that's the reason you're sticking around, why are you choosing to be in the same room?"

Just then, the canister falls to the floor. Evander picks it up and a crystal disk falls out. "How could I have missed this? It must have been stuck to the bottom of the canister and got jammed."

Kal'korg walks over and curiously asks, "What do you think is on it? It doesn't seem to be labeled."

Evander just shrugs and inserts the disk into another pad that is sitting on his desk. A recording of Evander's father plays.

Evander shrugs and inserts the disk into his pad. A recording of Evander's father plays.

"Day 159, Human day February 19ᵗʰ, 2990, continuing project Galgorn."

Evander begins to tear up as he hears his father's voice.

"We've finally been able to graph living tissue with the nanofibers and non-magnetic alloy skeletal structure."

Doctor Guryon starts going into details about creating Galgorn.

The nanobots, meanwhile, begin to morph again, prompting Angelica to attempt once more to assert control. "Halt and remain motionless!" she commands sternly. The nanobots promptly freeze in their tracks, having morphed into a metallic creature with big oval black eyes. The eyes are looking up at her expectantly as she turns back to the screen.

Evander can only observe the results with an amused sense of wonder, then he continues to watch the recording.

"...I have yet to tell Admiral Sarklak where I got the DNA sample from to form the organic flesh and tissue. If he ever found out that it wasn't from vetted and approved samples, I could get into serious trouble."

Evander pauses the recording. "This project must have been really important to him, if he was willing to risk his career."

Angelica chimes in, "Yeah, but whose DNA did he use?"

Evander shrugs and makes a suggestion of just watching the rest of the recording.

"If the Admiral ever found out that I used my own DNA to create the organic components, he might have me court marshalled or worse."

Evander immediately stops the recording again. Everyone's eyes widen from this revelation. The nanobots appear to mimic their expressions, with a mouth forming and gaping open as if surprised. Blarek points at the screen and says, "If your dad used his own DNA to make Galgorn, wouldn't that technically mean..."

Evander interrupts, and in a serious tone says, "That would make Galgorn technically my brother."

Kal'korg pipes in, "If your dad did use his own DNA, wouldn't that actually make him his clone?"

Angelica shakes her head and says, "Not exactly. Since his dad altered the DNA to allow it to bond with synthetic materials, this wouldn't make Galgorn a clone." She then looks at Evander. "Evander is more accurate—this would technically make him his brother."

Evander balls his fist and pounds it into his desk, causing the nanobots to start bouncing around.

"Great, not again!" Blarek gripes. "Hey Ange, since you seem to be able to control them, tell them to stop again."

Angelica tells them to stop and to stay still, but to no avail. "Okay, that didn't work."

Evander turns around, and in a serious, authoritative tone tells the nanobots to stop and do a diagnostic. The nanobots abruptly stop and go into a quick diagnostic mode, temporarily halting their activity. The eyes stare straight ahead, and the mouth has formed into a flat line, making the nanobots look like a robot shut down.

Kal'korg looks at them and says, "Quick thinking with the diagnostic thing."

The nanobots suddenly start to make a noise. "D...d....dia...dia...g....nost...ic....diagnostic com...plete."

Blarek looks at Kal'korg and then at Evander. "They can talk?"

Evander looks confused and says, "I didn't know either. I didn't realize they had the capability. I couldn't quite get that part to work properly."

Angelica chimes in, "Well, looks like they might have fixed that error themselves. By the way, maybe we should name them something else, rather than keep calling them nanobots. After all, they are acting like one entity now."

Evander, rubbing his chin agrees. Then Kal'korg turns and says in a childish tone, "And what would you name yourself, you malfunctioning error-ridden little guy?"

Angelica smacks him across the head and says, "It's not a child. What is with you?"

Kal'korg rubs his head, and in an upset tone, replies, "That really hurts, you know! And sorry, I just haven't had that much sleep lately, given what we've…"

The nanobots then started speaking again. "Ma… ma... Ma… llf… mall… Erro… Mall… Mall… Name… Mall… Erro… Name…"

Blarek smiles and snaps his fingers. "Why not Mal'Erro? It seems rather fitting don't you think?"

Evander ponders for a moment before saying anything, then replies in agreement. "Mal'Erro it is then. And you're right, rather fitting, considering I don't know if I can fix it or not, even if I wanted to." Evander kneels down and greets his father's creation, "Greetings Mal'Erro. You and I are going to be working together, sound good?"

Mal'Erro replies in a broken voice, "S…S…S…Sounds…goo…. go…good!"

Evander stands up and says, "And hopefully we can do something about fixing your speech. I think it might be that some of the nanobots are out of sync, but we'll deal with that later."

After the friends leave to return to their own quarters, Evander continues working on Mal'Erro. It has stopped morphing into different shapes and has settled on the form of a small robot about the size of a 5-year-old human child. It still has its large oval black eyes and small mouth, but has formed humanoid arms, legs, hands, and boots and a small protrusion on the center of its face to look like a nose. Its surface is an overall metallic grey with gold trim at each of the joints of its arms and legs. Finally, Evander climbs into bed, exhausted, but supremely satisfied with the results of the day. "Good night, Mal'Erro," mumbles Evan. Then he shuts his eyes and falls fast asleep.

CHAPTER THIRTEEN

The next day, Evander meets up with Angelica, Blarek and Kal'korg, to see Professor Heligan. The professor has a new type of holographic simulation he invited Evander to try out. "Greetings Evander, so glad you could make it and I see you've invited your friends as well." The professor smiles with delight. "Alright, Evander and Kal'korg, I want you both to help with some testing I need to do with my newest tweak to the training simulator. Angelica and Blarek, you can stay back here with me."

Evander and Kal'korg step together into the holographic simulation. It appears as a vividly dynamic fighting arena where their every move is mirrored by the artificial environment. Professor Heligan starts to give his instruction. "Alright you two, I'm going to test out the new sensation simulator. You are going to enter into a fight with each other and every time you get hit, you should feel some slight discomfort and maybe a bit of pain, but nothing to worry about, no actual harm will come to you . . ." and in a whisper to himself, he adds, "I hope."

Evander and Kal'korg look at each other and raise their eyebrows and just shrug. Two rapiers appear in front of them and each reaches to pick one up. Evander can feel the weight of the sword in his hand and the momentum of the slender blade as he swings it in the air.

The double edge feels smooth and sharp as he carefully rubs his finger along the surface. Professor Heligan then gives the command to begin. The clash of rapiers echo in the chamber as Evander spars with Kal'korg. Around them, holographic illusions add an element of unpredictability to the duel.

Angelica and Blarek watch from the sidelines, concern etched on their faces. With each contact from the holographic rapiers Evander can feel stinging pain and he can't escape the emotions that well up in his mind. The recent events, the activation of Galgorn, and the subsequent turmoil has left him grappling with conflicting feelings. Kal'korg manages to stab Evander in the chest, causing Evander to wince in pain. As the session continues, Evander and Kal'korg both exchange blows.

Meanwhile, Professor Heligan observes with keen interest, analyzing the efficiency of the holographic technology he has developed. The training session serves a dual purpose—testing the technological advancements and gauging Evander's and Kal'korg's combat abilities. Professor Heligan monitors the progress on his data pad, adjusting the settings as needed. Whenever he notices a hit, but no pain response, he makes some slight adjustments.

As Evander and Kal'korg engage in the simulated battle, the atmosphere in the holographic arena is tense, mirroring the weight on Evander's shoulders. Angelica and Blarek both exchange worried glances, sensing the internal struggle within their friend. As the session continues, it becomes clear to them that Evander is losing concentration. The professor doesn't really notice though, as his focus shifts to only the pain simulation, forgetting all about keeping track of Evander's and Kal'korg's abilities.

Just as they were about to hit each other one last time, the simulation comes to an abrupt halt and the holographic rapiers vanish. The ambient lighting shifts to an urgent yellow hue, casting an unsettling glow across the room. A stern voice echoes from the walls, calling for all available UPF officers. Everyone in the room stands up and listened keenly. Admiral Sarklak is commanding Lieutenant Angelica Tenah, Commander Eltrex, and all the officers in their crews to meet him in the briefing room.

Evander and Angelica exchange a quick glance, the camaraderie of the training session replaced by a sense of urgency. Without a word, they rush to the nearest pathway connecting the laboratory building to the command center. They quickly make their way to the briefing room, their footsteps echoing through the corridor. "I wonder what this is about. It's not often that two crews are called to the briefing room at the same time, especially on yellow alert," Evander says with a curious tone and expression.

Angelica just shrugs and says, "Whatever it is, it's definitely not good."

In the briefing room, Evander, Angelica, Kal'korg and Blarek meet up with Commander Eltrex and his crew. Angelica and Eltrex give each other a curt nod, then a holographic image of Admiral Sarklak appears. The tension in the air is palpable as they listen intently to Admiral Sarklak's holographic projection. The admiral's serious demeanor reflects the gravity of the situation.

"Officers," Admiral Sarklak begins solemnly, "we've received distressing news. There's been an attack on the planet Wap'lesia, which is known for developing advanced weapons and research. Our suspicions point to Galgorn as the orchestrator." Admiral Sarklak brings up the star map and continues, "The planet Wap'lesia is a very important asset to the UPF, as it's also where we get a majority of our armaments from."

The weight of the revelation hangs heavily in the room. Evander's thoughts race, grappling with the reality that his, essentially, estranged brother is potentially behind this devastating act. Evander doesn't want this to be his father's final legacy, one that others will remember.

The Admiral continues, "Lieutenant Tenah and Commander Eltrex, assemble your crews. Tenah - you will captain the Olympus

Starcruiser; Eltrex - the Thunderbird Celestial. You will go and investigate the area immediately. All other crews will stay vigilant for any signs of Galgorn."

Both Angelica and Commander Eltrex respond in unison "Understood, Sir!"

The Admiral's holographic image focuses on Angelica and says sternly, "And Tenah, although you are still in command, I go by a strict three strike system. So don't mess up this time." Turning his focus back to the group, he continues, "Now, stay focused officers. This is a critical mission."

As the holographic projection of Admiral Sarklak dissipates, the urgency in the room lingers. Angelica turns to her assembled team, determination etched on her face. "Evander, Kal'korg, Blarek, prepare for immediate departure, I'll inform the other officers of our crew to meet us at the launch center," Angelica commanded. "We're heading to Wap'lesia immediately. Time is of the essence."

The officers disperse, each member moving with purpose. Evander, though burdened by personal turmoil, finds solace in the familiar routine of preparing for a mission. His green eyes meet Angelica's determined gaze, silently acknowledging the gravity of the situation.

In the bustling activity of the briefing room, Ensign P'thorkia, the pilot of Angelica's crew, arrives and approaches her with eagerness, her purple tendrils seeming to dance. "I'm ready for action, Lieutenant! I apologize for being late," she exclaims, excitement dancing in her expressive eyes.

Angelica is happy to see the confidence in the young ensign and responds, "That's fine, just meet us all at the launch center. We're counting on you, ensign. Let's move out."

Angelica and her crew make their way to the Olympus Starcruiser, a formidable vessel ready to embark on a mission that will test their unity and resilience. As they approach the ship, Evander looks up at it in awe, admiring the slick design and flashy black and red paint job. The Olympus is one of the more advanced starships in the fleet. It has also recently been retrofitted with an advanced Dimensional Hop Drive (DHD). Evander can't help but always be awestruck by the sheer scope of the ship. It might not be one of the larger starships, but it is still capable of holding 70 crew members comfortably. Blarek snaps Evander out of his gaze and motions him to hurry up.

The team swiftly makes their way through the entrance and hurriedly prepares for the imminent departure. Angelica, now in her mission-captain's uniform, stands ready at the helm, prepared to guide her team through the impending mission. As Angelica sits in the captain's chair, she hears someone approaching her from behind.

Lieutenant Commander Froslo, the Calidorfian engineer known for his penchant for colourful language, approaches Angelica with an air of excitement. His gerbil-like features are contorted into a grin.

"Captain, you're in for a freakin' ride with this new DHD. It's a real piece of damn brilliant engineering," Froslo exclaims, his enthusiasm undiminished by the serious nature of the mission.

Angelica shoots him a bemused look. "Froslo, I appreciate your excitement, but let's keep it professional. We're on a critical mission here."

Froslo chuckled, his whiskers twitching with amusement. "Commander, you know me and my whole bloomin' species. Swearing is just a way we speak, even more so whenever things get bleedin' interesting. And trust me, this DHD is more than interesting—it's a goddam bloody marvel." Froslo then turns his attention to Ensign P'thorkia, who looks back at him with a nervous smile. "As for you, pilot, don't forget about the friggin' damn parking brake this time. With this being a flippin' larger vessel it will bloody-well be worse if you do!"

P'thorkia apologizes again and Angelica motions to Froslo to go back to engineering. Froslo mumbles to himself and glares at P'thorkia. The ensign just sinks into her seat and turns back around to the controls.

As Froslo returns to engineering, the team prepares for the dimensional hop, a blend of tension and camaraderie filling the air. Everyone on board is wondering what they'll find once they get to the planet and if they should be prepared for the worst.

Angelica keeps a level head, as she addresses the crew. "Prepare for a dimensional hop," Angelica commands as she punches in the coordinates for their destination. Upon clearing the atmosphere she gives the order, "Engage the DHD, Ensign P'thorkia."

Ensign P'thorkia, with confidence on her face, activates the DHD, initiating the creation of a transient wormhole. The ship's surroundings blur as they enter the opening, hurtling through the fabric of space. Moments later, they emerge near the troubled planet.

CHAPTER FOURTEEN

After arrival, Commander Eltrex, aboard the Thunderbird Celestial, volunteers to stay in orbit to survey the planet's vast expanse for any anomalous readings. His crew can sense his tension growing.

Angelica, determined to uncover the truth, lands the ship on the surface of Wap'lesia. The bustling weapons facility stands silent, the aftermath of Galgorn's swift and calculated intrusion. She exits the ship with some other crew members, including both Evander and Blarek. They spot some surviving employees, so they go to assist and question them. As she questions the employees, an unsettling truth emerges. Galgorn had an accomplice, someone matching the description of Jalerg.

Staying calm, she asks, "Thank you for the description. It does indeed sound like the suspect we're after." Taking out a pad that opens into a box with what look like windows on both sides, an image appears. "Just one last thing. Is this the person you saw?"

Angelica shows a holo-image of Jalerg, and the employees all acknowledge in agreement. Angelica thanks them for their time, but just as she walks away, one of the employees speaks up and mentions some of the peculiar items stolen. One item makes Angelica's face turn white. They tell her of a highly experimental missile. One that could enter a star's core. The missile itself is meant to only be a surveying device, but they inform her that with some modifications, it could be turned into a device that can destroy a star from the inside out. Angelica, for the first time ever, begins to shake. However, she quickly regains her composure.

She figures it will be wise to keep this revelation discreet, as to not cause a panic. She also thinks it best not tell Evander about Galgorn, given all that has happened. Angelica, armed with newfound intelligence, returns to the Olympus Starcruiser. The crew, now aware of Jalerg's involvement, braces for the impending threat.

Angelica strategizes her next move, as she ponders on where Galgorn might want to use that type of weapon. She goes in her captain's chambers, with the doors shutting behind her. She sits at her desk and slams her fist on the table. "What in the hell does Galgorn want with a weapon like that? What can he possibly gain from destroying an entire star?" Angelica keeps pondering on what to do next. The stage is now set for the next steps in this intergalactic chess game. Angelica, who is driven by duty and a desire to protect, decides it's best to move forward cautiously, mindful of the dangerous pieces on this cosmic board.

In his quarters, Evander is still grappling with the shadows of his past. The familial ties with Galgorn weigh heavily on his mind. He also knows there are concerns from Blarek, Kal'korg, and Angelica, creating an emotional backdrop to the mission.

Angelica decides to inform Admiral Sarklak of the progress she's making. However, before she can send a request, her monitor lights up. Admiral Sarklak is already reaching out to her for an update. "Lieutenant Tenah, I'm calling to see how the investigation is going?"

Angelica replies with a worrying tone, "Sir, the news isn't great. If what the surviving employees have told me is true, we might be facing an even greater threat."

After she tells him everything, the admiral urges her to stay behind and delve deeper into the investigation, to find out everything there is about this missile and if the other components stolen could be used to enhance the missile to its deadly capabilities. The admiral then mentions he's going to have Commander Eltrex return to base to prepare for the worst.

After the conversation ended, Angelica leans forward, as she grapples with everything that's gone on so far. She looks outside her window and sees a tiny flash of light in the sky—the Thunderbird Celestial going back to base. She wonders if the intricate components pilfered by Galgorn and Jalerg hint at a design beyond comprehension—a weapon capable of manipulating the very heart of stars. The chess game intensifies, as the pieces move across the galactic board, setting the stage for a confrontation that could alter the fate of the universe.

With the impending danger of the stolen experimental missile and its potential to unleash unprecedented destruction, thoughts begin to cast a long shadow over the mission. The crew's resolve will be put to the test.

While Commander Eltrex's ship hurtles through the cosmic tapestry on its way back to the base, Angelica remains on Wap'lesia, immersed in the gravity of the situation.

~~~~~~~~~~~~~~

Meanwhile in the clandestine depths of an undisclosed planet, Galgorn finalizes his sinister plans within the confines of an abandoned warehouse. Galgorn unveils a grand design — a new facility to manufacture a bio-android army. He knows of Jalerg's mechanical genius with a knack for biomechanics, which will play a pivotal role in this ominous venture.

Galgorn confers with Jalerg, "This missile is exactly what is needed. We should easily be able to duplicate it, as needed, and create an entire arsenal of solar destroyers."

Jalerg looks puzzled "I thought it was only going to destroy a star?"

Galgorn looks at him with disbelief. "Do you know nothing? If you explode a star from the inside, it creates a cascade effect that will essentially wipe out the entire solar system. Nothing will survive the destruction."

Jalerg raises an eyebrow and with a worrying tone, "What would destroying an entire solar system accomplish exactly? Or are you planning to destroy the system, then go and harvest the materials from it?"

Galgorn walks over to Jalerg and places his hands on his shoulders. "It's all part of a bigger plan that you don't need to worry about." Galgorn then removes his hand from his shoulder and walks toward a large desk. "Besides, we don't need to destroy all solar systems, we just need to create a large enough distraction for what's really coming next. The UPF, or even the entire galaxy won't know what hit them."

Jalerg begins to laugh and Galgorn continues, "As for you, do you understand what you have to do next?"

Jalerg responds with excitement. "Yes, I do. With the components we stole and the schematics that I also got before the poor doctor met his fate, I'll have a mass production facility ready to produce clones of you."

Galgorn grins with satisfaction. "Don't have them look like me completely. I want to be the only unique one. Except for two, I want two of them to look like me, after all, we have just begun to create havoc." Galgorn continues, "Now, I need you to head back to the planet, once the first duplicate of me is done. Is that clear? And contact our other friend. Let her know that the next part of our plan is well on its way, and she should be ready."

Jalerg's grin mirrors Galgorn's and he turns to carry out his orders.

~~~~~~~~~~~~~~~

Back on the Olympus Starcruiser, Angelica pours over the gathered data. The urgency of the mission weighs heavily on her shoulders as she processes the implications of Galgorn's malevolent ambitions. The stolen missile, a potential harbinger of cosmic chaos, becomes a focal point in her pursuit of justice.

While Angelica delves deeper into the labyrinth of information of the stolen inventory, Kal'korg is sitting with Blarek in the canteen area of the ship, discussing their growing concern for Evander. His connection to Galgorn, rooted in shared genetic material, adds a layer of complexity to an already intricate situation.

"I wonder what's going on in Evander's head, I'm really surprised he's even here on this mission after everything that has happened so far," Blarek says to Kal'korg in a hushed tone.

Kal'korg, twiddling his thumbs, replies, "I know what you mean, poor guy has gone through so much. I would say he has no family left, but he kind of does, in the form of a maniacal cyborg."

Blarek shakes his head and then tells Kal'korg in a serious tone, "That's not even remotely funny. I mean it's true in a way, but still not funny. Evander pretty much has nothing anymore, aside from us and that malfunctioning machine…"

"Galgorn?" Kal'korg interrupts, confused.

Blarek hits his face with a palm. "No! I meant the other malfunctioning machine—the one that is made of nanobots."

Kal'korg embarrassingly replies, "Oh yeah, I forgot about that thing. You know for a machine that is made of tiny little robots and doesn't work properly, it sure is a cute little guy. I wonder what its original intent was anyway."

Blarek shrugs. "Who knows? All I know is Evander has a lot on his plate and I'm not sure if he's taking the time to come to terms with all of it."

Kal'korg nods in agreement and both him and Blarek finish their lunch.

Amidst the silent hum of the Starcruiser's engines, while in standby and ready to leave the planet at a moment's notice, Angelica faces a pivotal moment. As the Olympus Starcruiser stays stationed on the planet, Angelica is acutely aware of the unfolding cosmic drama. The chase for Galgorn intensifies and the stolen missile becomes both a weapon of mass destruction and a key to unraveling the enigma that threatens the fabric of the universe.

As Angelica is mulling things over, she notices her screen buzzing. She answers it and Admiral Sarklak is on the other end "Lieutenant Tenah, we just got word of strange activities on a planet not that far from you. Since you're the closest, I want you to go and investigate it. I trust you got all the data you need?"

Angelica affirmed, "Yes sir, I doubt we can get anymore data from here. The last of the information about the experimental missile was just uploaded."

The admiral is pleased to hear this. "Excellent job Lieutenant. Keep this up and you might make Captain one day, despite your setback from earlier. I'm sending you the co-ordinates. Good luck Tenah." The call ends and Angelica tells everyone to get back into the ship and to prepare to depart.

CHAPTER FIFTEEN

The hum of the Olympus Starcruiser fills the air, as it gracefully descends onto the surface of Munaker Three. The planet stretches out below, a canvas of green, brown, and red, waiting to unfold its secrets. Despite the ship's advanced technology, the atmosphere inside remains charged with tension, a testament to the uncertainty of their mission on Munaker Three.

Angelica stands on the command deck, her gaze fixed on the holographic display of Munaker Three, with its barren landscape and three moons. The weight of her responsibilities as the mission captain presses upon her shoulders. Galgorn's elusive maneuvers and her lingering worries about Evander add an unusual layer of complexity to her decision-making. She thinks to herself, *"What am I going to do about you, my friend? It bothers me that I cannot help you more and I know you need time to sort things out."* She begins pacing. *"Was it wrong of me to allow you to join us? And what about Galgorn? What is that monster planning? Hopefully we'll find answers here on this planet, even though I do wonder what he was doing here in the first place. It's not exactly a paradise and there's no real strategic advantage to be had here."*

This internal struggle is a novel experience for Angelica. Throughout her career, she had seamlessly separated her personal life from her duties. Now, with the stakes higher than ever, she finds herself questioning the boundaries she once took for granted. Angelica internally screams, but her face, remains calm and composed. Throughout her life, she has always known what to do, but now… she's unsure.

~~~~~~~~~~~~~

In a quieter corner of the ship, Evander is lost in thought. *"Dad, Mom, I miss you both so much. What am I to do? I know Galgorn isn't truly related to us, but in a way, he is."* Tall and sharp-witted, his green eyes reflect a mixture of caution and curiosity. He runs his fingers through his brown hair, as he contemplates the upcoming mission. *"Will I truly be able to confront Galgorn? Knowing now that he's, by all rights, related to me? I'm afraid that Galgorn won't come in without a fight. A fight that will be the end for one or both of us."* Evander heads to his quarters, still thinking things over. He knows his friends are worried and are there for him, but Evander also serves as Angelica's second-in-command, a role that has thrust him into the forefront of this unfolding drama. Should he have not accepted?

Ensign P'thorkia, the hyperactive and loyal pilot of Angelica's crew, notices Evander as he walks inside his quarters. She senses Evander's unease. She sees Kal'korg and approaches him.

Kal'korg's listens intently as P'thorkia expresses her concern about Evander. His protective instincts kick in and he responds, "Evander is struggling, but he'll let us know if things aren't alright." Without saying it out loud, he adds to himself, *"at least I hope he does."*

With a comforting smile from Kal'korg, P'thorkia is reassured — an unspoken testament to the bond among the crew members.

Evander, Blarek, and a team of officers assemble in the hangar wearing the ULTRA suits. Each officer carries the weight of their specialized skills and the uncertainty of what awaits them on Munaker Three. Angelica wishes them all luck and reminds them again to be careful, as they do not know what to expect. Then she gives them a rare salute. They all salute in return and get inside a land transport vehicle that has two large tires on the front and treads on the back.

The airlock hisses open, and the team drives onto the alien landscape. Munaker Three, bathed in an otherworldly glow, presents an aura of both beauty and danger. Angelica's voice resonates through their communication devices, providing mission directives and emphasizing the importance of caution. "You're to investigate and find any evidence of Galgorn being here. If you do find evidence, I want you to make sure you also find out what he was doing." Evander acknowledges and ends the call.

Strange readings emanate from the planet's surface, guiding the team toward an abandoned structure—an ominous relic of the past. The tension builds with each step, and Evander's keen instincts are on high alert.

Blarek, jokingly points at the structure and says, "They must've had one heck of party. Don't you think?" They all look at him and laugh. Everyone except Evander. One of the crew remarks, "Well then, if we're lucky, we might find some left over party supplies." Blarek looks over at Evander, hoping to see a reaction, but there was nothing. They finally reach the abandoned building, which looks extremely rundown and covered in foliage.

Inside the structure, the team discovers remnants of Galgorn's presence. The air is thick with a sense of foreboding, as they navigate through abandoned corridors. Suddenly, a holographic projection of Jalerg materializes before them. An unexpected antagonist who anticipated their arrival. "I see you finally arrived; we were hoping someone would show up."

Jalerg, with a twinkle in his teal eyes and brushing his emerald-green hair aside, taunts the team with a sinister grin. His arrogance permeates the holographic image, as he brags about his recent adventures in the service of a mysterious benefactor, all while hinting at a deadly surprise. "Did I forget to mention? I'm working with Galgorn now and we've been hard at work. I must congratulate you—you lot get to be test subjects for our newest creations all based on a familiar design."

Just then, five beings appear, almost from nowhere. Evander sees them all wearing a cloaking watch, similar to the one Jalerg was reported to have stolen. He now wonders how long they were watching them. Before he can finish his thought, a scuffle ensues when the quiet corridors come alive with the mechanical whirring of Galgorn's modified cyborgs. These creations, eerily similar to Galgorn, but enhanced with additional weaponry, present a formidable challenge.

"Blarek, behind you!" Evander yells, as he see's one of the cyborgs coming up behind Blarek, who gets knocked forward. Everyone takes out their weapons and the fighting continues. One of the officers gets stabbed in the shoulder, while another gets kicked into a wall. The cyborgs are relentless in their fighting. To make matters worse, they're having trouble keeping track of them, as they keep using the cloaking watches.

Amid the chaos, Evander's focus wavers. He locks eyes with one of the cyborgs, detecting an unsettling resemblance to his father—a revelation that momentarily paralyzes him. The emotional impact reverberates through the scuffle, adding a layer of complexity to the unfolding drama. Evander thinks to himself, *"What am I doing here? Father why did you have to go and make Galgorn out of your own DNA?"*

Suddenly the cyborg, who was bemused by Evander's hesitation, begins to lunge at him, blade in hand. An officer, seeing Evander standing motionless, steps in front of him to ward off the cyborg. The blade pierces his armor and hits his heart. Evander suddenly snaps out of his trance and screams! Evander, in a fit of rage, takes out his gun and sword. He attacks the cyborg with everything he has. He finally manages to destroy it, after firing his gun in it's face.

Meanwhile, Blarek and the other remaining officers are holding their own. They manage to destroy two more cyborgs, but at a cost. Another officer got seriously injured, losing his arm in the scuffle.

The fight ends when two cyborgs manage to escape the skirmish, leaving the team with the casualties. Blarek, with his protective instincts in full force, tends to the wounded officers. The loss of one team member hangs heavily in the air, casting a somber shadow over the mission. "Damn it! I can't believe we just walked into a trap like that." Blarek angrily growls. Evander sits on a nearby bench, still traumatized by the death of the officer.

The hologram of Jalerg reappears, delivering a chilling ultimatum, "I hope you don't think this was the end of the fight." He reveals that the building is rigged to blow. Blarek looks at a cyborg's remains flashing and suddenly realizes that the cyborgs themselves are rigged to blow when defeated. Evander, Blarek, and the remaining officers rush out just in time, narrowly escaping the violent explosion.

Outside, with the debris settling, Blarek carefully checks on Evander. The worry in his eyes reflects the toll the mission has taken on the team. "Evander, are you sure you're okay? What happened back there? Why did you freeze up?"

Evander just looks at him with tears welling up in his eyes that he quickly wipes away. "I…don't know, I honestly don't know, just that it's my fault that officer was killed. I should have been the one that took that blade to the chest, not him."

Blarek just pats Evander and hugs him. He then tells him he's going to go check on the other officers, but that he'll be back shortly. "Also, I'm going to have to ask for pick up. The debris from the building wrecked our vehicle. Froslo is going to have a field day with this." As they wait for extraction, Blarek reflects on the events that unfolded on Munaker Three, aware that their journey has only just begun.

CHAPTER SIXTEEN

The Olympus Starcruiser echoes with the weariness of recent events as Blarek, Evander, and the remaining officers return from Munaker Three. The weight of emotional turmoil settles over Evander, his medium build reflecting the invisible burden he carries. The loss of a fellow officer hangs heavily in the air, casting a somber shadow over the crew. No one was expecting such a thing to happen, especially with finding out that Jalerg is now working with Galgorn. As everyone arrives and exits the extraction vehicle, Evander looks back out onto the planet. Guilt and remorse riddling him, driving him into even further despair.

Blarek, seeing the expression on Evander's face, places a reassuring hand on Evander's shoulder, attempting to ease the guilt that threatens to consume him. The ship's corridors, once filled with anticipation, now resonate with the echoes of their mission's failure. Blarek sees Kal'korg charging in, with relief on his face upon seeing Blarek and Evander both in one piece, but then sets his sights back to the injured officers.

Kal'korg, takes charge of the injured officers, guiding them to the medical bay for care, where the chief medical officer is waiting for them. Meanwhile, Blarek and Evander make their way to the command deck.

While walking, Blarek asks Evander, "So how are you holding up? You can't blame yourself Evander. With everything that's been happening lately, it's a wonder you're still holding it together."

Evander just keeps looking ahead. "I know Blarek, but I wonder how the admiral or even Angelica will see it. After all, if it wasn't for my hesitation, that officer would still be alive."

Blarek shakes his head and stops him for a moment. "Evan, just remember that no matter what happens, we all have your back. You're one of our best friends after all." This makes Evander give a glimpse of a smile. However, the air gets thick with unspoken tension as they continue their approach to the command deck. Both Blarek and Evander head toward Angelica's office.

In the captain's office, Angelica waits for a debrief on the mission. The information unfolds, revealing the events on Munaker Three, as a potential trap. After the debriefing, Angelica, now grappling with the gravity of the situation, asks Evander to stay for a private meeting.

Evander diverts his gaze as Blarek looks pleadingly at Angelica, who says in a serious tone, "Thank you Blarek for the debriefing and good job out there. Now I would like a private word with Evander, so please go to your post."

Blarek, feeling more helpless than he has felt in a long time, sits down at his console. The door closes and Blarek starts to worry. He's never known Angelica to be so strict with her friends before, even though he understands she must show some authority, as the mission-captain.

Behind the closed doors, Angelica's demeanor changes. The weight of command settles on her shoulders, as she confronts Evander. The atmosphere is tense as Angelica, now more than a friend, reprimands him for losing focus during the mission. "Evander, I must say, I am very disappointed in you and the way things went." Evander lowers his head in shame. Angelica informs him that the injuries and the death of their fellow officers are on his shoulders. As she reprimands him, the captain's office becomes a crucible of emotions.

Angelica, who values the bond with her crew, can't help but let her frustration surface. The air in the room crackles with the intensity of the moment. "How could you allow yourself to lose focus like that? This isn't like officer training, and you are no longer a cadet. This is the real world, with real consequences." She stands up from her desk and folds her arms. "Look I know you and I are friends, and this is new territory that you, me and the others are going to have to get used to. You and I both know I have no choice but to write you up for this."

Evander shamefully nods his head in agreement without looking Angelica in the eyes. With a regretful expression, Angelica looks at him and says more gently, "Evander, I know others have talked to you already, but I must say, I'm deeply concerned. You have not taken the time to grieve or to process everything that has happened." She starts walking around her desk, then leans on the front of it, looking at Evander. "I honestly am sorry, for everything that has happened. For the loss of your father, for the surreal realization that Galgorn is partially related to you and the trauma of going through something similar again that happened to your mother, but I truly need you to try and get your head on straight, please!"

Evander looks up at Angelica and angrily yells, "As I keep telling everyone, I am perfectly freaking fine!" He slams his fist down on the table beside Angelica.

Angelica is taken aback as she has never seen Evander snap back at her like this. She rights herself and in a calm and commanding voice says, "Evander Guryon, you can leave my office immediately and go cool off!" Without any further comment, Evander turns and leaves her office.

Angelica takes a few minutes to regain her composure and leaves her office, stepping onto the command deck. She informs everyone on the bridge that she's going to her quarter, leaving Blarek in charge. Her expression, despite her attempt to hide it, reveals the internal conflict of being both a friend and a commanding officer. As she walks down the corridor, she walks past the med bay and sees the injured officers being treated. One of them is being fitted with a prosthetic arm. After reassuring each one individually, she exits and proceeds to her quarters.

In the solitude of her room, regret lingers. Angelica understands the necessity of her actions, yet the personal cost weighs heavily on her conscience. The line between friendship and command blurs, leaving behind a bitter taste of responsibility. *"What am I going to do? I shouldn't have said what I said to Evander about his mother and father."* She goes and lays down in her bed. *"How am I going to explain this to the admiral in the report? 'Oh, and by the way, my friend and second in command is having emotional problems, after suffering from potential PTSD, not just losing one parent to a lab accident, but to another. But he's fine, he'll get over it.'"* She sits up on her bed and leans forward, placing her hands to her side. *"Yeah, that will go over well. I just wish Evander would stop bottling things up. He might not realize it, but if he keeps doing that, eventually he's going to explode. And when that happens, I'm afraid I'll lose a good friend."* Angelica walks over to the sink and splashes some water on her face, continuing to try and think things through.

Meanwhile, in the training bay, Evander seeks solace in the rhythmic sound of punches meeting a training target. Each blow serves as a physical manifestation of his internal struggle and pain. The weight of Angelica's disappointment, the regret he feels from how he acted in her office and the burden of the lost life of a fellow officer hang heavy in the air. The emotions and trauma for him keep piling up. Even he doesn't know how much more he can take.

With every strike, Evander grapples with the haunting questions: Could he have done more to prevent the tragedy on Munaker Three? If he was in the lab with his father and Kes, would things have turned out differently? What did he do wrong that prompted Kes to break up with him in the first place? The training bay becomes a sanctuary for reflection, a space where emotions are expressed through controlled violence. Evander keeps punching the training target, harder and faster, letting out his anger and frustration. Since he didn't wrap his hands, his knuckles begin to bleed, but he fights through it. He figures he deserves this, that he deserves the pain. Internally he yells, *"What could I have done differently? Why did my father have to make such a machine in such a manner?"* Evander hits the training target harder and harder. His knuckles leaving bloody prints on the training target.

With one final swing, Evander lets out a loud scream, hitting the target as hard he can. He then collapses in front of it, keeping his head down. Going over and over the events that have happened, not knowing how to move past them. He understands that he's worrying his friends, but he doesn't know what to do or even where to begin. Years of being bullied, years of emotional pain, never letting it out completely. Never expressing his true emotions. So, in the silence of the training bay, alone, he just stays kneeling on the floor in front of the training target, quietly weeping.

As the Olympus Starcruiser sits stationed on the planet, the aftermath of what happened lingers. The crew, bound by the intricacies of friendship and command, faces the challenges ahead. The scars of the recent mission run deep, leaving them to navigate the uncharted territories of the cosmos. Throughout the ship, everyone is feeling a sense of dread and unease.

CHAPTER SEVENTEEN

The weight of the recent events presses heavily on Evander's shoulders as he navigates the ship's corridors, the echoes of Angelica's disappointment still reverberating in his mind. He looks down at his hand and he decides to make his way to the med bay, to get his hands looked at before heading to his quarters. While heading there, he thinks that the cathartic exercise would have provided some kind of relief, however it does not. It more so dulls the pain. The ambush on Munaker Three, the cyborg that bared the resemblance to his father, the loss of a fellow officer, and Angelica's disappointment persist in the recesses of his mind. No matter how hard he tries, he can't stop thinking about. But for now, he's able to once again bottle it up, suppressing his emotions.

Unbeknownst to Evander, as he is heading to the med bay, Angelica is around the corner and sees him coming down the corridor. She doesn't want to face him just yet, so she stays hidden out sight. Concern lines her features as she witnesses the impact of her harsh words on her friend. Regret begins to build within her—a gnawing uncertainty about whether she was too harsh, knowing that Evander wasn't in the right mindset for such a mission.

Angelica had believed that field duty might have offered Evander an escape from the internal struggles he faces. *"I'm sorry my friend,*

I thought I had made the right decision." Now, witnessing the toll it has taken on him, she questions her decision. Wondering if her attempt to help has, in fact, caused more damage, Angelica grapples with the fine line between leadership and friendship.

After getting his hands taken care of, Evander leaves the med bay and heads toward his quarters. Kal'korg comes out of the med bay, exhausted and worried. He notices Angelica. "Hey Angelica, what are you doing hiding?"

Angelica embarrassingly admits, "I was actually avoiding Evander. I think I might have pushed him a bit too far. I should have been a bit more understanding instead of putting even more stress onto him." She then regains her composure and asks, "Is he doing okay by the way? I didn't know he was injured from the attack—I thought he was fine?"

Kal'korg informs Angelica in a hushed tone, "No he wasn't injured from the attack. I mean, in a way he did get injured in an attack, but I highly doubt a training target would attack back…unless they were given an upgrade to do so? They weren't, were they? I don't want to see more officers coming into the med bay for a while."

Angelica looks confused. "He got injured from a training target?"

Kal'korg responds quietly, "Yeah, I guess he was trying to blow off some steam and went a little to hard on the training target. He ended up cutting his knuckles. He did say he cleaned up the mess before coming here." He chuckles, "At least I was able to do some dermal repairs on him. Unfortunately, between you and I, I feel he needs more help than you or I can possibly provide."

Angelica responds sadly, "I know. I just wish he would open up a bit more. I mean, I get it that he wants to try and keep things bottled up and he tries to put on a smile, but I think things are starting to be a bit too much, even for him." Angelica informs Kal'korg that she's heading back to the command deck, and she'll talk to him later.

In the midst of Evander's internal battle, the ship's vastness becomes both a refuge and a prison. The pulsating hum of the Olympus Starcruiser is a backdrop to the intricate complexities of relationships among the crew. Froslo is busy looking over the wreckage of the wrecked vehicle, Blarek is sitting at the controls next to Ensign P'thorkia. Angelica walks onto the command deck and notices Evander is not there. She checks to see where he is and she is informed he was last reported heading toward the hangar.

Spurred by a determination to make amends, Evander decides to revisit Munaker Three's debris field. His initial mission was marred by chaos, but perhaps a closer inspection can yield data and evidence crucial for tracking down Galgorn. So, he decides to go to the hangar and take one of the smaller vehicles, with just enough equipment and storage. He also takes with him some snacks, just in case.

"There must be something remaining there, perhaps some remains of the cyborgs. If I can find something, it might help provide clues as to where Galgorn is. Not only that, but maybe, if I can find an intact memory core of the cyborg, it might help us in figuring out what he's planning," Evander thinks to himself.

Meanwhile, Angelica brings up the video feed of the hangar and she observes Evander's departure. She decides to give him the space he needs. In her mind she thinks, *"I hope you stay safe Evander and I hope you find what you're looking for."* Understanding the gravity of the situation, she grapples with the consequences of her actions. The captain's responsibility weighs heavily on her shoulders, as does the friendship she shares with Evander.

Blarek gets up out of his chair and walks up toward Angelica. "Are you sure you don't want to send anyone with him? What if he gets attacked again?"

Angelica reassures him, "I don't think anyone is there still, I strongly believe they set that trap for any UPF officer, just to test things out. Isn't that what Jalerg told you?"

Blarek sighs, "That's true. I'm just worried that's all. You didn't see him out there. It was as if he was in a totally different universe. I just hope he's safe out there."

Angelica leans forward in her seat and then looks up toward Blarek. "I hope so too, but I think he needs his space right now. Don't worry, if anything does happen, I have officers on standby to help, just in case."

Angelica's response puts Blarek a bit more at ease. He then asks, "So any word about how we should proceed?"

Angelica leans back into her chair. "Nothing yet. For now, all we can do is wait and analyze whatever data was collected." Angelica looks back at Blarek. "If you want to, you can take a break for a bit until we hear something." With that Blarek, heads to the galley for a much-needed break.

~~~~~~~~~~~~~~~~~

At the remains of the building, now rubble, Evander arrives. He gets out of his vehicle and grabs his equipment. He walks around and begins to search for anything that might be useful. Evander digs through the rubble for a few hours. He is about to give up, when he suddenly spots something shiny. He goes over to the area and begins to dig. To his excitement, he finds the partially damaged head of a cyborg and, as he checks it over, he sees the memory core. To his disappointment, it's too damaged. He is about to give up when he notices a second area in the cyborg's head that's enclosed. Curious, he opens it up and finds an intact memory core in good condition. He figures it must be a back up, just in case something happens to the first. He takes it out, safely tucks it away, and continues looking around.

As Evander sifts through more of the wreckage, collecting samples and examining potential evidence, an unexpected movement in the skies above catches his attention. Another spacecraft zooms overhead and a familiar reading pulses on his equipment—the same signature detected within the building on Munaker Three.

With his curiosity piqued, Evander double-checks the data. Realization strikes him like a bolt of lightning—this could be the very ship that Jalerg and the cyborgs arrived in. Evander prepares to defend himself, but after seeing no immediate threat, he stands down. He's now convinced that this is a crucial lead in their pursuit of Galgorn, so Evander wastes no time informing Angelica of his findings. He runs to his vehicle and opens communications with the ship. Angelica calmly asks him for his report, which catches him off guard. He thinks for sure that he is going to get into a lot of trouble for leaving without permission. Putting his confusion aside, he proceeds to inform her about the situation and what he's found.

He apologizes to Angelica for leaving without permission, and then he shares the fact that he found an intact memory core and some other pieces of evidence that might be useful. Lastly, he tells her of his revelation about the mysterious spacecraft that flew overhead. Angelica, in her role as captain, acknowledges the significance of the information and orders Evander to return to the ship immediately.

With a sense of urgency, Evander gathers the evidence and equipment, his mind now focused on the larger mission. The debris holds secrets, and he's determined to unravel them, even if it means facing the consequences of his earlier actions. As he's packing up his stuff, he sees the craft again. It's almost as if it is taunting him. What could it possibly want? As Evander makes his way back, the shadows of Munaker Three linger, but with what he's gathered, he's hopeful it will point them in the right direction.

CHAPTER EIGHTEEN

Now that his search for new evidence on the planet over, Evander feels the effect of his adrenaline rush wearing off. He trudges back to his vehicle with his things, his mind haunted by the disturbing discoveries in the abandoned facility. Packing up the evidence and equipment into the vehicle, he forges ahead, driven by the unwavering sense of duty that guides his every step. As he gets the last of the stuff loaded, he thinks, *"Let's hope that ship hasn't gotten too far. I'm positive that ship was the one Jalerg and the cyborgs are on."* Evidence in tow, he presses down on the acceleration peddle, to get back to the ship as soon as possible. Behind him a trail of dust and dirt is being kicked up by the tires, as he rushes back.

Meanwhile, aboard the Olympus Starcruiser, Angelica grapples with her own thoughts. Anticipation brews as she awaits Evander's return, wondering how he'll cope with the aftermath of their mission. She gets lost in her train of thought, not noticing at first the communication console blinking on and off. It is signaling an incoming message from Admiral Sarklak, who is injecting a new layer of urgency into an already tense atmosphere.

Angelica addresses the admiral, "Sir, what can I do for you? If you're looking for my report, I'll have it ready for you as soon as Evander returns from his data recovery mission."

The mission, of course, is unknown to the Admiral Sarklak and he raises an eyebrow. Disregarding this information for the moment he responds in a serious tone, "Lieutenant, I'm calling on a few things. First is to inform you, that we analyzed the data of the equipment Galgorn had stolen. It appears none of it is meant to be used to enhance the missile but is in fact usable in the creation of more cyborgs, potentially like himself."

Before the admiral could finish, Angelica interjects, "I think we have just seen firsthand that it's more than just usable sir. Galgorn managed to do so."

Admiral Sarklak, with a worried expression, replies, "I don't think I want to wait for your report, Lieutenant. You might want to tell me immediately what has happened."

Angelica proceeds to inform him of the details. After listening, the admiral tone is grave. He replies, "I see, so the whole thing was a trap to test these new cyborgs out. I'm sorry for the loss of one of your crewman Lieutenant Tenah."

Angelica gives a slight nod of her head in acknowledgment, then replies, "Thank you sir. I must admit, I do feel responsible for the officer's death."

This prompts the admiral to interject. "It's never easy to lose a crewman under your command. I've lost people as well, but the key thing to do is to keep moving forward and not to let it get to you. They knew what they signed up for and what the risks were. So, it's best not to blame yourself and I know that's easier said than done."

Angelica reflects for moment on what he said. "I understand sir, I'll try my best. If you don't mind, might I ask what the second reason for this call is?"

Admiral Sarklak expression turns serious again. "Very well Lieutenant. The other reason for this call is to inform you that you're to come back to base with any evidence you might have gathered. Also, we've found some more data about those nanobots. Turns out they were supposed to enhance the ULTRA suits, as well as provide extra support when needed. But unfortunately, the doctor couldn't fully complete the project. It was something he and his wife were working on together before that unfortunate accident. Furthermore, there was more data, but it appears it was corrupted. We have people working on the recovery of it." The admiral leans back in his chair and continues, "If we can get it up and running, this might be a real asset for the UPF. Now, I'm curious, has Evander made any progress on fixing it, by any chance?"

Angelica leans back in her chair. "I'm afraid not Admiral. I must confess, he's been going through things, and I felt it best not to pursue the matter until he's ready." She leans in toward the monitor. "However, if you wish, I can order him to work on it."

The admiral shakes his head. "No, that won't be necessary. Just get back to base with all the evidence you've gathered and have the report ready." With that, the communication ends. Angelica makes a ship wide announcement. She informs them that Admiral Sarklak has ordered them to return to the base. Everyone is to prepare for departure.

Angelica knows that with the data collected, particularly insights into the nanobot designs from Evander's father, it could be a pivotal asset for the UPF. The mission's success is measured not only by what was discovered on Munaker Three, but by how this newfound knowledge can shape the future.

The crew, including Kal'korg, Blarek, and Ensign P'thorkia, carry a collective sense of apprehension. As friends and allies, they share the burden of the unknown. The ship hums with activity as preparations for departure are underway, a silent acknowledgment that the next steps could unravel the mysteries surrounding their recent endeavors. In engineering, Froslo gets his people to prepare.

Upon returning to the ship, Evander keeps thinking he is going to be met with another reprimand, however, instead of a reprimand, he is greeted with an unexpected embrace from Angelica. Her demeanor shifts, a moment of levity injected as she jokes about his unauthorized sample collection mission. "I hope you were able to get good evidence. Otherwise, I will change my mind about not writing you up."

Evander replies with surprise, "Wait your not writing me up? I'm somewhat confused now."

Angelica just laughs and tells him to go to his post. Proving that the camaraderie between them, a testament to the bonds forged in the crucible of their shared missions, remains unbroken.

Before Evander takes his position on the ship's command deck, Angelica shares the latest findings. The readings from the mysterious spacecraft align with previous encounters, pointing to the presence of a Phosingian, possibly Jalerg. The enigma surrounding Galgorn and his elusive cyborg creations, adds complexity to the puzzle, intensifying the sense of impending danger. "We analyzed the data from before and the data you sent over about the ship. It's indeed possible that ship belongs to Jalerg. Why was he lingering around? We're not sure, but we haven't been able to find the ship again on our sensors."

Evander scratches his head. "They might still be out there, after all we didn't pick up anything when we arrived. We were even ambushed by those cyborgs that appeared to have the cloaking watches added into themselves." Evander sighs, "Must be a gift from Jalerg to help solidify his partnership with Galgorn."

Angelica agrees, "I think your right." Angelica, bearing the weight of her command, also reveals information recovered from the investigation into the lab accident. "There's one other thing as well. The data concerning Mal'Erro, which was previously believed to be contained within the canister, proves to be incomplete. They found more data that survived in the lab explosion. Turns out, Mal'Erro was meant to help enhance the ULTRA suit. However, there seems to be more data that was corrupted, so it's not all complete. There's a team that's trying to recover it. Hopefully, they'll be able to do so."

Angelica informs him that they were given orders to return to the base with all the collected evidence. "Let's hope we don't run into any more trouble." Angelica's brow furrows and she ponders, "I think it's troubling that we weren't able to detect the ship. How could they have gotten past our sensors with out detection? And why would a ship, with the same signature as the one we got from the building, just appear and stay in plain view? It doesn't make any sense."

Evander shrugs and says, "That's a good question. I felt like it was trying to taunt me, as though it wasn't expecting to see me there and I have a good feeling that it's not done yet. I'm also curious about that corrupted data." With the revelation of incomplete data, it leaves Evander with questions, but he knows that time is of the essence and the journey back to base now becomes a crucial step in unraveling the mysteries entwined in their mission. With the looming threat of a star-destroying missile somewhere out there, they must find it before Galgorn can weaponize it. Or even more terrifying, if it already has been weaponized, then before it can be used and then replicated.

As the Olympus Starcruiser begins to initiate its departure, the crew braces for the unknown that awaits them. From chasing down a murderer, to now hunting an escaped cyborg with a missile that's able to create devastating havoc and destroy countless lives, it's now more important than ever to find Galgorn and Jalerg. Everyone on board is wondering what Galgorn plans to do with more cyborgs like himself. With more questions than answers, the ship with its crew heads back to the UPF headquarters.

CHAPTER NINETEEN

As the Olympus Starcruiser gracefully slips into orbit, the crew's attention is drawn to the same spacecraft that Evander previously saw flying the skies from the planet's surface. A collective curiosity fills the ship, and Angelica, ever inquisitive, attempts to establish communication with the enigmatic craft. The silence that follows is disrupted by an unexpected turn of events—the craft, seemingly inconspicuous, unleashes a volley of lasers toward Angelica's formidable ship.

Confused, Angelica commands, "Ensign Guryon, try hailing them."

Evander tries, but also questions "Captain, why are we trying to hail them? Why not just destroy them, considering they already fired on us?"

Angelica in a serious tone, "I want to give them a chance before doing that. They clearly must know that they aren't going to be doing anything to us."

Evander keeps trying to hail the ship. The crew, however, are puzzled by the audacity of a seemingly inferior craft attacking their powerful vessel. They watch as the lasers prove futile against the Olympus Starcruiser's shields. Angelica, maintaining her composure, observes the spectacle until the craft takes a more aggressive turn, firing a neutrino torpedo. Once it hit, it bypassed the shields, damaging the outer shell of the ship.

Furious Angelica yells out "What in the hell! Ensign P'thorkia, damage report?"

Ensign P'thorkia responds "Ma'am, we have fires on decks 2 and 3. We also have a breach on the port side of deck 2."

Angelica's patience wears thin, and she swiftly orders Ensign P'thorkia to pursue the assailant, with Blarek preparing for potential retaliation. "Can't say we didn't give them a chance, lets end this quickly. Ensign Ta'yash, prepare to fire on my command." Blarek nods in acknowledgment.

As the pursuit unfolds, the situation escalates unexpectedly. More crafts emerge, their markings revealing the ominous insignia of the Red Novas, a notorious pirate organization led by the formidable pirate queen, Lyritha Quorlon. The peaceful orbit becomes a battleground as the pirate ships join the assault, turning a routine mission into a desperate struggle for survival.

"What in the world? Ensign P'thorkia, Ensign Ta'yash, how did we not detect them?" Angelica worriedly questions. This prompts the two officers to shrug their shoulders.

Blarek in a panicky tone "Captain, it's possible they integrated the invisibility technology into their ships. That might be how they're going undetected. The same thing happened down on the planet when we got ambushed." Blarek helps maneuver the ship. "Our sensors, at the time, didn't detect anything; not until they weren't invisible anymore."

Evander suddenly realizes that he was wrong. The extra slot wasn't a fried memory core, but a fried invisibility device and the device attached to the cyborgs that he thought was for invisibility, must have been how they activated it.

Angelica, swift in her decision-making, calls for arms and orders for the launch of the fighter crafts to bolster their defense. Officers start to board the crafts and prepare to launch. The ship continually vibrates under the onslaught, and Lieutenant Commander Froslo, with his engineering team, works tirelessly to maintain the integrity of the shields. While working on one of the conduits for the shields, one of the engineers gets seriously injured when it explodes.

Meanwhile, during the chaos, Evander steps forward, volunteering to board a fighter craft. Angelica, a mix of pride and concern in her eyes, approves his departure, watching him go with a worried expression etched on her face, "Just be careful and try to come back in once piece."

Evander grins and replies, "I might not be great with the sword, but I do know my way around a spacecraft, plus Blarek showed me a few moves." Angelica covers her face with her palm and looks at Blarek who just shrugs. The ship continues to vibrate from being hit. Evander's ship launches and immediately goes to work firing at the hostiles.

With explosions and weapons firing everywhere, Evander evades them. He's successfully hitting the enemy ships and destroying them. A neutrino torpedo narrowly misses him but hits one of the ships in front of him. A piece of debris hits his ship, and he bangs his head on the console, knocking him unconscious.

Amidst the ongoing battle, Jalerg, the ever-arrogant murderer, intrudes upon the ship's communication system. "Hello everyone, I'm sure you're wondering how I highjacked your communications and why am I taunting you? You see, the test wasn't done, the cyborgs were just the beginning. We needed to see how well the newest additions to the ships, which were so graciously donated to us by the lovely people of the Red Novas, would fair. I must say it's going gloriously!" His laughter taunting everyone, as the onslaught continues.

"I would stay, but as I just mentioned, this is only a test for things to come, and I must say, it passed with flying colors. So, until next time." Jalerg abruptly ends the communication. The pirates, following Jalerg's lead, create a wormhole using a Dimensional Hop Drive, signaling the end of their assault. All the pirates start to withdraw, leaving behind wreckage and destruction.

As the pirates withdraw, Angelica orders the return of all remaining fighter crafts. The ominous truth dawns upon her—they were manipulated into this confrontation. It wasn't just a random attack—it was all a trap. Galgorn has orchestrated it all, just to test out new technology. *"How close is he to completing the weaponization of the missile?"* she wonders. The realization that he is close weighs heavily on her and she begins to worry. As she does so, she gets reports on the casualties. Fourteen UPF ships destroyed. On board, another four killed and twenty seriously injured. Angelica asks if Evander made it back, but was informed, he did not. Fearing the worst, both her and Blarek look at each other with worry.

Angelica communicates with the entire ship, "First, I want to say you all did a great job. Secondly, we did lose good people today in the line of duty. They died with honor, fulfilling their duties. They will be missed, and their memories will live on. We took some heavy damage, but thanks to them, we're able to make it home…"

Froslo interrupts from engineering. "Blimy, Captain, I don't mean to interrupt, but I thought you should bloody-well know something."

Angelica stops her communication with the entire ship. "Lieutenant Commander Froslo, what is it? I was in the middle of something important."

Froslo, in his usual colorful language, in helping with accentuating his urgency, reveals that there was damage to the DHD during the skirmish. "I just thought you should know, we aren't going any dodgy place fast, friggin' literally in fact." He mentions that repairs are imperative but will take a day or two. Angelica, acknowledging the situation, urges him to try for swift repairs, cognizant of the need to return to the central headquarters.

Froslo in his usual manner responds, "I'm an engineer, not a damn bloody miracle worker. If you want that type of thing, then might I f…." Angelica cuts him off before he goes into a swearing tirade. Shaking her head, she decides to just go and sit down.

Suddenly, Ensign P'thorkia Turns around and says, "Captain, there's another small ship approaching, it's one of ours."

They get a communication request and upon opening a channel they hear, "Hey everyone, what'd I miss? Sorry I'm late getting back, but I have a massive headache, and I guess I needed a nap," Evander, who survived, says jokingly.

Angelica gets up and rushes to the hangar. With the immediate threat neutralized, Angelica greets Evander upon his return, expressing pride in his performance. "I thought you were dead, I'm so relieved that you managed to survive."

Evander jokingly says, "Yeah, so am I. Although now I have a massive headache. By the way, shouldn't you be on the command deck?"

Angelica gives a grateful look and replies, "Yes I should be, but I'm your friend also and I was worried that you didn't make it." She then invites him to her quarters for a private conversation amidst the ongoing repairs and the ship's recovery from the unexpected assault. "But first, go to the med bay to get your head checked out."

"I get it, I'm not in the right headspace," Evander jokes.

Angelica just shakes her head. "No, not that type of head examination." Evander grins and informs her that he'll see her later after he gets a check up.

Later, inside her quarters, Angelica extends an apology for her earlier harsh words. "I hope you can forgive me Evan, I let my anger get the better of me and I must admit, this is all new to me. I never had to juggle between friendship and being in charge. It is difficult being in command of other officers, especially when one of those officers happens to be my friend, who I'm worried about."

Evander, understanding the challenges, reassures her, "It's alright Ange, I get it. I'm not in the right headspace, now more than ever. Apparently, I have a concussion."

Angelica and Evander laugh. They then delve into a conversation that spans the night, bridging the gap between command responsibilities and the enduring camaraderie forged amidst the trials of interstellar conflict.

The ship's crew either settles for the night or engages in repairing the damages from the attack. For now, all seems serene, and the crew members have a chance for some respite.

CHAPTER TWENTY

A few weeks pass without any further incidents, creating an illusion of calm within the cosmic turmoil. The crew are back at the UPF central headquarters. Galgorn and Jalerg seem to have vanished from the radar, allowing a deceptive tranquility to settle over them. Amidst this veneer of serenity, Evander finds himself struggling to cope with the lingering shadows of past encounters. His friends, particularly Angelica, notice the toll it takes on him, prompting concerned discussions among the crew.

In the galley area, Kal'korg is sitting with Blarek, Ensign P'thorkia and Angelica. Blarek looks at Angelica and in a hushed tone asks, "So what are we going to do about Evander? I hate seeing him torturing himself like this?"

Kal'korg places a hand on Blarek's shoulder. Angelica looks at them and responds, "I don't know, but for now, the best we can do is give him space. Don't forget everything he's just been through. First, the only thing he needed to worry about was the breakup with Kes. However, now he has to work through three more things: his father's and Kes's death and the revelation that Galgorn shares his father's DNA, which does make them related, in a way." Angelica sighs, while looking down. "I understand what that's like having to make a choice between doing the right thing and not hurting a sibling."

Everyone at the table looks at her. Ensign P'thorkia, in a soft tone, asks, "Did you have to arrest or put down a relative before?" Everyone looks at Angelica with curiosity, as she doesn't speak much about her past.

Angelica looks at them and says, "It was a long time ago, ancient history you might say, but I did have to make a hard choice." Looking up at the ceiling while reminiscing she continues, "It's something I don't like getting into, but let's just say, when the time came, I couldn't bring myself to harming them." Angelica wipes a tear from her face. "Anyways, it was a long time ago. But as I said, I can understand what Evan is going through and I feel he just needs time to heal."

Kal'korg says, while also having food in his mouth "You know…if he keeps bottling his feelings away…. like he always does…" He swallows his food. "He's never going to be able to do so. Also, he's started spending most of his time in his quarters these days, working on that malfunctioning machine nanobot thing."

Blarek responds in agreement, "That's true. How can he expect to heal, if he doesn't actually slow down and take the time? If he isn't there, then he's rushing off on missions with us. I know we gave him a choice and he always accepts, but if this keeps up, we might end up

with him losing focus again and it might be him that gets killed."
Everyone at the table goes silent.

Kal'korg breaks the silence. "Maybe since you out rank him
Angelica, you could command him to work on himself? You know,
force him to have some R&R, so he can try and get past this."

Angelica shakes her head. "Even if I did, that would most likely
just add more to his already full plate and that might break him
irreversibly. I can't watch him do that." Angelica hesitates for a
moment. "Although, you did give me an idea. I'll need to go talk to
Doctor Isa. As a physician and a psychologist, she might be able to
help him. I'm surprised that he hasn't gone to see her yet."

Blarek laughs, "Most likely because he figures she would give
him a shot and he absolutely hate needles, just as much as he hates
bugs." As he takes a drink he says, "Like remember the time during
training, we had another cadet that looked like an arachnid and how
much he freaked out when he had to spar with him?"

Kal'korg nods and smiles in agreement. "I remember that I never
saw him run so fast. I also never saw a door swing open in the
opposite direction before either."

Ensign P'thorkia, with a curious expression, says, "I thought doors either went to the side or went up? I didn't realize there were any doors on the training base that swung open."

Blarek looks at Ensign P'thorkia with a big smile. "Your right, they don't. But he was also wearing an ULTRA suit at the time and even with that, he still ran right into the door and straight to his quarters. It took maintenance an entire week to fix that door."

Angelica laughs and says, "I remember that." She then calmly and more seriously gets back to the matter at hand with their friend. "Either way, we must try and convince him to go on his own to see her. I don't think we can just force him to go." Everyone at the table agrees.

~~~~~~~~~~~~~~~

Meanwhile, Evander, in his quarters, remains haunted by the recent events, especially the escape of Jalerg's craft, possibly with Galgorn on board. Engrossed in his work on Mal'Erro, the nanobot creation of his father, he finally achieves a breakthrough. Mal'Erro begins to speak with less stutter, a promising development that temporarily distracts Evander from his own inner turmoil.

"Finally, I think I figured out the problem with your syncing program for your voice. You shouldn't be stuttering anymore. Can you say something Mal'Erro?" Evander asks curiously.

Mal'Erro looks at Evander. "Hello Evander, I think you did fix the problem. Hurray, no more stuttering for me. Thank you!" Mal'Erro excitedly turns into a ball and roles around the desk and then morphs back into a humanoid miniature robot. "This feels...gr-gre...at!" Mal'Erro stops, realizing it's stuttering again.

Evander reassures it. "Well, you still have a bit of stuttering, but for the most part, it's not too bad. I'll keep working on you." Evander goes back to work on Mal'Erro.

Mal'Erro analyzes the look on Evander's face. "What's wro...ng Evan? You still look...sa...ad."

Evander puts down his tools and gives a long sigh. "It's fine Mal'Erro, it's just a long day." Mal'Erro can tell that's not the case but decides not to push the issue.

~~~~~~~~~~~~~

Blarek, Kal'korg, and Angelica walk down the corridor toward Evander's quarters, still worried about Evander's ongoing struggle. They decide it is time for an intervention and come up with an idea.

They knock on his door and as he welcomes them in, he proudly showcases the progress he has made with Mal'Erro. However, his friends are more concerned about him than the technological advances. They suggest a visit to a nearby bar, an attempt to divert his mind from the burdens he carries.

"We're all heading out for a drink at that bar nearby the base. We won't take no for an answer from you either. We miss hanging out with you, so hurry up and get changed." Blarek says while nudging Evander's shoulder. "Who knows, you might find someone else there as well. Huh?"

Evander tries to dissuade them, trying to come up with an excuse. But before he can continue Angelica interrupts and says, "Didn't you hear him, we aren't taking no for an answer. So come on and get into some cleaner clothing. The drinks are on us!"

Mal'Erro, ever observant, stammers out it's approval for Evander to go, assuring him that it will be fine. Evander keeps insisting that he's still busy and looks over at Mal'Erro. The little robot informs him that it'll be fine and that he should go. Evander, unable to find a good excuse, finally reluctantly agrees. He reminds Mal'Erro to recharge itself while he is away and to stay in its room, better yet in it's cannister. To this, Mal'Erro salutes and agrees. The others exchange puzzled glances at the unusual interaction between Evander and the nanobot creation before leaving for the bar.

As Mal'Erro sees them leave, it begins to roll around the room. It playfully whistles and bounces up and down on the bed. It then goes and plays on Evander's computer for a bit. As it's playing, it hears a curious noise out the door. It knows Evander told it to stay in this room, but curiosity gets the better of it. It opens the door and sees Admiral Sarklak walking down the hall, talking to another officer. Hesitant, Mal'Erro sneaks out of the room and follows him.

~~~~~~~~~~~~~~

At the bar, the atmosphere is lively, but Evander remains somewhat closed off. Blarek, attempting to lift his spirits, assures him that their bonds are unbreakable, and they will stand by him through thick and thin. A brief smile graces Evander's face, but it quickly fades, replaced by a lingering concern.

Angelica puts her arm around him. "Come on Evander, loosen up a bit. You're at a bar with friends, at least try to show a bit of enthusiasm?"

Everyone else murmurs words of acknowledgment, and they all lift their glasses. "To Evander," they all say in unison. Then Angelica adds, "To our best friend, who we all care for and admire and to whom we would lay our lives down for." After hearing this, Evander gives a smile with a tear, because hearing the last line reminds him of what he's lost.

Ensign P'thorkia walks over to him and tries to comfort him. "You might have your quirks about you, but you're not a bad person. Just try to remember that we're all here for you." Everyone else agrees and Evander smiles again, albeit forcibly.

CHAPTER TWENTY-ONE

Back at the base, Mal'Erro is still curiously following the admiral and the other officer, until they part ways upon reaching the admiral's office. The admiral enters his office, and just before the door closes, Mal'Erro follows unnoticed.

Looking up, Mal'Erro accidentally gives out a high-pitched whistle. This alerts the admiral to Mal'Erro's presence. "What in the name of...What are you doing here little guy? I thought Evander was still working on you?" The admiral reaches out his hand to scoop up Mal'Erro, which startles the little robot, and he jumps out of reach.

The admiral reassures it that he isn't going to hurt it, but Mal'Erro starts to frantically bounce around the room. This prompts the admiral to try and catch it. Mal'Erro desperately tries to find an exit, but to no avail, and in a stutter "You'll never...catch me alive copper, yeah...see!"

The admiral stops trying to catch it, watching while Mal'Erro is still bouncing around. "What in the worlds has Ensign Guryon been programming you with, or for that matter letting you watch?" The admiral again attempts to try and capture Mal'Erro.

187

Back at the bar, Angelica suggests a visit to Doctor Isa, a proposal that Evander promptly dismisses. "I'm fine, I swear I am," Evander insists, resisting the idea of seeking professional help.

Kal'korg intervenes, expressing the collective worry of their friends. "Evan, you're not fine, we're all worried about you. You lost focus during the mission, and you keep to yourself most of the time in your quarters when not on missions or training."

Both Blarek and Ensign P'thorkia agree. Angelica then tells him in a calm, serious manner, "We're your friends Evan and we all care about you. We just want to make sure you're fine. Please go visit Doctor Isa tomorrow. Do it for us!" They keep on insisting that Evander pay a visit to Doctor Isa. The concern etched on their faces prompt Evander to reluctantly agree. He promises to see the doctor the next day.

Angelica gives Evander a hug. "Thank you. We just want to make sure you're okay, and whatever happens next, we'll be by your side as much as possible." She kisses him on the cheek. "First thing in the morning, I'll let Doctor Isa know you'll be stopping by."

Kal'korg chimes in. "That's right, we'll always have your back Evan. You've always been there for us, even during the time in training when my pants caught on fire, and you offered me the spare from your bag. Sorry about putting a hole in them, though."

Evander with a smile says, "Thank you everyone, I really do appreciate it. Come on let's enjoy the rest of the night." Everyone cheers!

~~~~~~~~~~~~

Back at the admiral's office, Admiral Sarklak is a bit out of sorts. His uniform is uncharacteristically untucked with him sweating. He starts to feel like he's a new cadet going through drills. The office is turned upside down, as he tries to look for Mal'Erro, whom he lost track of.

In the corner ceiling of the office, Mal'Erro, who manages to change his shape and blend into the surrounding area, looks on at the admiral. Once scared, it now thinks this as a game. Mal'Erro doesn't even notice that its power is almost drained. The admiral yells, "Come here you idiot machine! That's an order!" Two officers open the door, prompting Mal'Erro to stealthily leave the office.

One of the officers ask, "What's going on sir? Is everything alright?"

Admiral Sarklak, in an angry tone, responds breathlessly, "Yes it's fine, I'm just looking for a…" realization strikes as he notices the door still open, "…a shapeshifting machine, which I think just escaped this room. I'm going to kill that blasted thing."

One of the officers speaks out, "If it's the same machine that Ensign Guryon was working on in his quarters, I believe he calls it Mal'Erro sir." This prompts the admiral to glare at him. "Sorry sir. Would you like us to help find it?"

The admiral gives a sign of affirmation. "Find it and then roast it! It's a damn menace. I don't even know why I allowed that officer to continue working on it!" Just as the officers are about to leave, they hear a loud thud down the corridor. All three look out and see a puddle of metallic type of goo on the ground.

The admiral walks over. "Finally ran out of juice, huh?" With a smile and a low chuckle, he asks the officers to scoop it up and put it back into Evander's quarters. The officers acknowledge the admiral's request and proceed to do so.

Once getting to Evander's quarters, they spot the cannister, place Mal'Erro into it and close the lid. "There you go little guy," one of the officers says softly. "You really made the admiral mad and made a mess of his office, didn't you?" He then leans in a bit more and whispers, "Do it again sometime?" He gives a sly wink and both officers exit the room, leaving Mal'Erro to recharge in his cannister.

~~~~~~~~~~~

The following day, after Evander wakes up, he looks over at the cannister. He decides to leave it alone and head toward Doctor Isa's office. As he's walking, he sees the admiral's office door open and workers coming in and out. He then sees Admiral Sarklak coming out and greets him with curiosity, "Good morning, sir. What happened to your office? Are you doing some renovations to it?" Evander is obviously unaware of what transpired the night before.

The admiral looks at Evander and was about to say something, but a worker comes out of the office and runs into the admiral. The admiral just tells Evander to carry on, as he goes back to what he was doing. Evander shrugs and continues on his way.

Once at Doctor Isa's office, he hesitantly knocks on her door. The door opens, revealing a pristine space, full of light and plants. On one side, she has an examining table. On the other side, a couch and chair with a coffee table and some books. Her desk separates the two areas, and two chairs sit in front of her desk. She sees Evander and welcomes him in. "I was informed by Ms. Tenah of your arrival. It seems you have a lot of your friends worried about you." She informs him about a few mental tests she would like to conduct to assess his fitness for duty.

"These won't take long, Evander. Please take a seat on that couch over there and we'll begin with a few questions." As she instructs him in a calming and soothing voice, she motions toward the couch.

Evander, nervously asks, "There aren't going to be needles involved is there?"

Doctor Isa tells him not to worry. "That isn't the type of tests we'll be performing. I'm just going to ask you a couple of questions. Then later I'm going to have you put on that special cap over there," she says, pointing toward another chair with a type of helmet that resembles a mix of a strainer and a hockey helmet. Evander just gives a tilt of his head in agreement and sits down.

A couple of hours pass and Doctor Isa invites him over by her desk. "Just give me a few moments to go over the results. It shouldn't take long."

Many moments later, Doctor Isa puts down her glasses. "Evander, unfortunately, the results indicate that you're suffering from PTSD, post traumatic stress disorder, and severe depression. I'm sorry to say, but I'm going to have to let the admiral know." She then orders him to take a few months off. She calmly tells him, "It's for the best I'm afraid. You need to take time to heal from all this emotional trauma. Although I agree, working on that…working on Mal'Erro might be helping to a degree, you're still running out doing missions.

You haven't stopped to give yourself time to grieve. Now it might take you some time, everyone grieves in their own way, but you should take as much time as you can."

Frustration and denial well up in him as he argues against the test results. "The results have to be wrong. I'm perfectly fine. I don't need to be pulled off duty. If it's because I've been losing focus lately, I can do better and I will."

Doctor Isa, with a mix of empathy and professionalism, urges him to accept the necessity of a break, citing the accumulated trauma he has endured. "I'm sorry Evander, but in my own professional opinion, you need to take time off. In order for you to do better, you need to get better first. I'm sorry, but I have a duty as well, and I must order you to take a mandatory leave of absence from duty. Go on a vacation or go visit your family home that you mentioned during the session. That might help the healing process and help you move on. Again, I'm sorry, but it truly is for the best."

Dejected, Evander leaves the office with a heavy heart. While walking back to his quarters to start packing, Doctor Isa's words resonate with him, acknowledging that everyone had a breaking point, and his has finally arrived. The weight of past experiences, the recent encounters, and the burden of command has taken their toll on him. As he contemplates the mandatory break, a shadow of sadness clouds his usually determined gaze, signaling a struggle within that extends beyond the cosmic battles he faces.

CHAPTER TWENTY-TWO

As the news of mandatory time off sinks in, Evander returns to the solitude of his quarters. The weight of recent events presses heavily on his shoulders, as he contemplates this new unexpected turn of events. A decision forms in his mind—a return to his roots—his childhood home on Tesamer Five.

The journey down memory lane begins with the familiar sights and sounds of his family home. The walls echo with the laughter of his parents and their shared moments creating a vivid tapestry of love and warmth. The aroma of his father's culinary delights wafts through the corridors, bringing back the comforting memory of blueberry French toast, adorned with powdered sugar, whipped cream, and chocolate sauce. His mother's subtle sighs in response to his father's culinary extravagance are etched in his mind, a bittersweet melody of a time long past.

His childhood home, though modest, exudes a sense of grandeur fueled by the love and care that once resided within its walls. With each thought, Evander is transported to a time when life was simpler, and happiness seemed boundless.

With a new resolve Evander embarks on the task of packing, preparing for a journey, not just through space, but through the recesses of his own memories. *"Perhaps the Doctor is right and maybe this is for the best. Although, I can't just sit idly by with Galgorn still out there, along with Jalerg."* As he keeps thinking to himself, he's opening drawers and taking out his clothes, packing them into his duffle bag. The memories just keep coming, like a dam that finally gives way and bursts.

As Evander sifts through his belongings, his hands brush against a worn envelope tucked into the corner of a drawer. He hesitates for a moment, his heart heavy with anticipation and longing. The words penned by his mother dance before his eyes, each stroke of the ink carrying her essence, her love, her unwavering strength. His gaze lingers on the phrase *"Open when things look dire, love mom!"* It is a tender reminder of her enduring presence, even in her absence.

With trembling fingers, he carefully unfolds the letter. The soft rustle of paper echoes in the stillness of the room. As he begins to read the letter, it's as if her voice resonates in the depths of his soul. Each word he reads is guiding him through a labyrinth of his emotions. Memories of her gentle touch and her soothing lullabies wash over him like a gentle breeze, wrapping him in a comforting embrace.

Dear Evan,

If you're reading this, things must be pretty tough right now. No matter what, I want you to know that I love you more than words can express. Life can throw some crazy curveballs our way, but it's how we handle them that defines us.

If I'm not around anymore, know that my love for you will always be with you, guiding you through the ups and downs of life. I can't imagine what you're going through, but I believe in you, Evan. You've always been my shining star, my little miracle. Your dad and I went through a lot before you came along, but you were worth every second of the wait.

You've taught us so much about resilience and strength, and I hope you never forget that. Even when things seem hopeless, remember that you're capable of amazing things. Within you burns the light of a thousand stars, a celestial brilliance born from the union of love and hope. You've got this incredible light inside you, Evan, a spark of love and hope that shines brighter than any star in the sky.

So take your time to heal, to reflect, but never lose sight of that inner fire. Let it guide you through the darkest nights and lead you toward brighter days. Know that no matter where life takes you, my love will always be right there beside you.

With all my love and faith in you,

Mom

Her love for him radiates from every word. In that moment, Evander feels her presence beside him, her warmth enveloping him like a protective shield. His heart swells with gratitude and a profound sense of loss. Yet, amidst the ache of her absence, he finds a glimmer of hope, a flicker of light to guide him through the shadows. Though she may be gone, her love remains etched in his heart, a guiding star to illuminate his path.

Evander sits down on his bed while holding the letter. The letter not only continues the memories, but also gives him a reminder to not give up hope. He knows he needs to get over what's going on and what has happened. He knows he needs time to heal in order to be back to his normal self. Somberly, he sends out a silent thought, *"Thank you Mom and Dad."*

Amidst the process and his thoughts, a gentle knock on the door causes him to stir from his thoughts and look toward it. The door glides open, with Angelica on the other side. She steps in, having heard the news, and a heartfelt conversation ensues.

"I'm sorry you're being made to take some leave, Evan. I wish there was another way, but you know we're all worried about you, right?" Angelica says while taking a seat beside him.

Evander looks at her. "I understand, although I still don't believe I should—not with Galgorn and Jalerg on the loose still." With a frown of discontent, he gets up and continues to pack.

Angelica, ever the caring friend and leader, shares words of understanding and support. She continues to assure Evander that the decision for him to take time off is for the best, echoing the concerns of all his friends who wish for his healing. "I get it, trust me I do. If I was in your shoes, I wouldn't be able to go with unfinished business either." She gets up and walks toward him, placing her hand on his shoulder. "But you've been through so much and you haven't really taken the time to process or to heal."

Her words resonate with truth, and he knows she and his other friends mean well. "I know, and trust me, I want to be better. I want to be able to move past all this, but I find it very hard to do so. I don't even know where to begin still."

Angelica sighs and with a smile looks at him. "Why not begin with relaxing? You've done nothing but work on Mal'Erro and gone on multiple missions, almost nonstop. I'm amazed that you're even fully awake right now." She takes her hand off him and while folding her arms, says, "You need to do this Evan, because I'm afraid if you keep going on like this, you might end up seriously injured or worse."

Evander, grappling with the tumultuous emotions within, appreciates the genuine concern of his friend. "I get it Ange; it's never been my intention to make you all worry about me." He puts the stuff he is holding onto the table and continues, "But what am I supposed to do? My dad died, my girlfriend broke up with me and then she died the same day. Then we had that disastrous mission where I ended up causing…"

Angelica cuts him off, "Evan, that officer's death wasn't your fault. Sure, you lost focus, but he did what he needed to do to protect a fellow officer. Who knows, maybe it would have still ended up the same way, even if you hadn't lost focus." Angelica hugs him. "Please, try and understand that. There really wasn't anything else you could have actually done in that moment. Everyone knew what the risks were when they joined the UPF."

Evander sighs and says, "It just hurts so much, to the point my heart feels like it wants to leap out of my chest. I feel like I have to constantly fight with my own mind just to stop thinking about it, even for a split second."

Angelica hugs him again, tighter, then lifts his chin and stares into his eyes. "Just take the time Evan. Take the time to heal, eventually you'll get better. The pain might not go away completely, but you might be able to cope with it much easier and better."

Angelica then offers her assistance in packing, a gesture he accepts. As they work together, Evander continues to open up, expressing the weight of the burden he feels. In the company of his closest friend, Evander unveils his struggles—a tapestry woven with threads of loss and the unrelenting pursuit of justice. Angelica, a beacon of empathy, listens contently, understanding the depth of Evander's pain.

"I really wish you would learn to not bottle things up so much, Evan. Maybe it might help you more, if you let your emotions free occasionally, instead of internalizing all the time."

Evan acknowledges his tendency to internalize emotions—a coping mechanism honed since the tragic loss of his mother.

As the sorting and packing progresses, Evander reaches for the canister housing Mal'Erro. He activates it and Mal'Erro spills out, forming quickly into its little robot self. Evander tells it, "We're going to be going on a vacation. We're going home, so I can relax—but I promise you that I will still dedicate time to continue working on you."

Mal'Erro responds with enthusiasm, "My first trip away from this place? Thank you! I swear I'll be on my best behaviour, but I hope we aren't gone to long, someone asked me to help with Admiral Sarklak."

Angelica and Evander looked puzzled. "What does the admiral need help with?" Angelica asks confused.

Mal'Erro just bounces around, prompting Evander to get it back in it's cannister. Once back inside, Evander closes it. Angelica just shrugs and says, "I guess we'll find out later what it meant by that."

Later on, after having everything all packed up, Angelica and Evander head toward the launch center for Evander to catch a lift to his family home. Upon arrival, Kal'korg and Blarek are waiting. Kal'korg greets him with a sly smile. "Hey, we're going to miss you while your gone, but I do have something for you." Kal'korg points toward a medium ship. It has the words *Kunvive* written on worn bold letters.

Evander looks shocked. "Is it on the ship?"

Kal'korg shakes his head. "Nope, it is the ship—belonged to my granddad, who left it to me in his will. It's the Kunvive, which means 'a center of companionship'. I never use it, especially since I have one already, and I felt you could make use of it. It's more of a camper ship anyways, but with modified weaponry on it and good shielding." Looking at it more closely he adds, "Not the latest or best shielding, but it's still good in a pinch, in case you run into pirates or xenophobic extremists."

Evander can't believe it! He hugs Kal'korg. "Thank you, my friend, I'll take good care of it."

In the final moments before his departure, Evander bids farewell to Angelica and the rest of his friends. Angelica reassures him that they will visit whenever possible. The three friends, with their arms linked around each other, stare on while Evander boards the Kunvive. After turning and waving, Evan closes the door and heads to the helm, then sets a course for his childhood home. The engine hums with a mixture of nostalgia and anticipation, carrying him away from the cosmic turmoil to a place where healing might begin.

CHAPTER TWENTY-THREE

In the desolation of a hidden planet, obscured in the untouched realms of the galaxy, Jalerg is working away finishing preparations for the arrival of an important guest. Galgorn, the cybernetically enhanced mastermind, immerses himself in the unfolding of his malevolent design. Surrounded by screens and connected by a cord attached to his neck, Galgorn methodically reviews memories extracted from his legion of cyborg drones; their collective consciousness stored in the central hub.

While watching, he hears the screams of a thousand people. *"The plan is going perfectly. Soon it will be time to enact the rest of it,"* Galgorn with a menacing grin, thinks to himself.

As the memories dance across the screens, painting a tapestry of calculated brutality, Galgorn turns to acknowledge the arrival of his guest—Lyritha Quorlon, the enigmatic leader of the Red Nova pirates. Her tendrils of hair framing a visage of determination. "Nice set up you got here. Very…moody," Lyritha says, her voice dripping with sarcasm.

Seated regally upon a chair forged from the remnants of conquered technology, Galgorn exudes an air of calculated power as he considers the pirate queen. His mechanical throne, adorned with the gleaming relics of battles past, serves as a stark reminder of his dominance in the realm of technology and conquest.

As he rises, the machinery inside him whirs softly, a symphony of gears and circuits echoing his movements. With a sardonic twist of his lips, Galgorn regards Lyritha, his gaze sharp and penetrating. "Your presence is... unexpected," he remarks, his tone laced with a hint of amusement. "Though I must admit, I did entertain the possibility of your arrival. After all, our alliance is not one easily dismissed."

The room crackles with tension as Galgorn takes a step forward, his towering figure casting a shadow over Lyritha. Despite the coldness of his metallic exterior, there is an undeniable charisma to his presence, a magnetic pull that commands attention. "Shall we proceed to matters of mutual interest?" he inquires, his voice dripping with an air of intrigue. "Or shall we indulge in pleasantries first?"

Lyritha's mannerisms are sharp and decisive, a testament to her unwavering determination. She replies, her voice tinged with a hint of impatience, "The sooner we conclude our business, the sooner I can return to the sea and resume my endeavors." There's a glint of anticipation in her eyes, a hunger for action that mirrors Galgorn's own.

A shared moment of mirth passes between them, a rare instance of camaraderie amidst the weight of their alliance. Their laughter echoes through the chamber, a fleeting respite from the gravity of their circumstances.

Turning his attention to Jalerg, Galgorn issues his commands with a cool authority; his words carrying the weight of command. "Leave us and continue your review," he instructs, his tone firm yet measured. "Ensure that our soldiers are prepared for what lies ahead."

Jalerg, ever obedient, acknowledges the directive with a curt nod before departing to carry out his orders.

In a dimly illuminated chamber, Jalerg presides over another array of screens displaying the vivid and unsettling memories of both the cyborgs and Galgorn himself. Amidst the chaotic collage of images, one particular memory file draws Jalerg's attention like a moth to a flame. "Well, well, what do we have here?" he muses aloud, his curiosity piqued by a repeated playback of a single memory.

As Jalerg delves deeper into the memory file, a sense of unease creeps over him, like tendrils of darkness coiling around his consciousness. On one of the screens, a scene unfolds with chilling clarity—a moment frozen in time, replayed over and over again. Galgorn, with a sinister gleam in his eye, relives the harrowing act of ending Doctor Guryon's life, each viewing seemingly more gratifying than the last.

A shiver of apprehension courses through Jalerg's frame as he grapples with the implications of this disturbing revelation. What significance could this particular memory hold for Galgorn? Why does he revisit it with such chilling fascination? These questions linger in Jalerg's mind, casting a shadow over his thoughts.

Despite his growing unease, Jalerg steels himself, determined to press forward with his assigned task. With a resolute silent affirmation, he banishes his doubts to the recesses of his mind, refocusing his attention on the present moment. There are tasks to be completed, duties to fulfill, and Jalerg will not allow himself to be deterred by lingering doubts or unsettling discoveries. With unwavering resolve, he returns to his work, methodically attending to his responsibilities before turning his attention to the next item on his agenda.

~~~~~~~~~~~~~~~

Back in the main chamber, Galgorn's shadow dances ominously across the walls. The unholy triumvirate convenes for their clandestine meeting. Seated amidst the labyrinth of screens adorned with cryptic data, Galgorn assumes the role of a dark puppeteer orchestrating the discourse with a calculated air of authority. Across from him, Lyritha exudes a palpable aura of defiance, her eyes gleaming with a fierce determination as she meets Galgorn's gaze head-on.

"I must say, phase one of testing went very well," Galgorn remarks, his voice a low rumble that reverberates through the chamber like distant thunder. "I'm also very pleased with your crew's performance. They did exceedingly well."

As the conversation unfolds, Galgorn delves into the intricacies of their collaboration, probing Lyritha for insights into the effectiveness of the enhancements bestowed upon their ships. "They worked marvellously," Lyritha responds, a sardonic smirk playing at the corners of her lips. "No one even saw us coming."

A ripple of dark amusement courses through the chamber as Galgorn and Lyritha exchange banter laced with veiled threats and sinister implications. "I must admit," Lyritha muses, her tone infused with mock sincerity, "when you came to me with this offer, I was tempted to gun you down myself." Lyritha leans in, her expression a mix of defiance and amusement. "Now I'm glad I didn't," she retorts, her laughter mingling with Galgorn's in the murky depths of the chamber. Together, they revel in the twisted camaraderie born of their unholy alliance, each word spoken echoing with the weight of their shared ambitions and dark desires.

~~~~~~~~~~~~~~~~

In the depths of his hidden laboratory, Jalerg presides over his dark domain with a mixture of pride and trepidation. Surrounded by the eerie glow of flickering monitors and the steady hum of machinery, he surveys the sprawling expanse of his macabre workshop. Here, within the bowels of the cavern, lies the heart of their operation—a relentless assembly line churning out an army of biomechanical monstrosities, each one a testament to Galgorn's insidious vision.

As Jalerg peers into the abyss below, his gaze falls upon the vast fleet of ships acquired through their covert dealings with the Red Novas, a silent testament to their ambition. The walls of the cavern are lined with endless rows of tubes, each one containing a nascent cyborg in various stages of development. With meticulous precision, Jalerg oversees the assembly of his unholy creations, each one a twisted amalgamation of flesh and machine.

"I still can't believe the efficiency of this," Jalerg murmurs to himself, his voice echoing faintly in the dimly lit chamber. "Each new cyborg, helping to make new cyborgs. Endlessly increasing the supply to this ever-expanding army."

As he scrutinizes the data streaming across his monitors, Jalerg's attention is drawn to two special tubes nestled among the countless others. Within them lie two exact replicas of Galgorn himself, their lifeless forms a chilling reminder of the depths of his master's ambitions. With a furrowed brow, Jalerg ponders the significance of these creations, a sense of unease gnawing at the edges of his consciousness.

"What are you up to?" he mutters under his breath, his gaze lingering on the inert figures within the tubes. Despite his expertise in biomechanics, Jalerg finds himself haunted by the enigma of Galgorn's intentions; a shadowy specter lurking just beyond the reach of his understanding.

~~~~~~~~~~~~~~~

As Galgorn and Lyritha stand amidst the pulsating screens, the air crackles with anticipation, each word exchanged laden with the weight of their ambitions. With a confident smirk, Galgorn casts a glance at Lyritha, his gaze ablaze with determination. "As long as we stick to the plan, things shall go smoothly," he asserts, his tone laced with unwavering conviction.

Lyritha, her expression cool and composed, her eyes gleaming with the promise of conquest, replies, "Oh, I agree," With her voice dripping with icy resolve she continues, "When we're done, the UPF will either surrender or they'll be wiped out. I can see all that loot now. Me and my crew will be set for the rest of our lives and then some." Lyritha, though harboring reservations about the enigmatic Galgorn, shakes off her uncertainties, motivated by the allure of promised riches and power.

Galgorn's laughter rings out, a chilling echo in the cavernous chamber. "Oh, you'll get your fill of loot alright," he chuckles, the sound reverberating against the walls. "There will be so much that you'll need a second or even millions of extra ships to help haul it all."

As Lyritha departs, her laughter mingling with the echoes of their conversation, Galgorn's gaze returns to the myriad of screens before him, his mind already consumed with thoughts of conquest and domination. The ominous ambiance intensifies as Galgorn summons Jalerg, instructing him to test the capabilities of the burgeoning cyborg army and prepare the first solar killer for deployment.

In the depths of the cavern, where shadows dance with the echoes of sinister machinations, Galgorn's eyes glow with an otherworldly red. The alliance, a marriage of convenience fueled by greed and clandestine objectives, sets in motion a cataclysmic tide that surges toward unsuspecting worlds, heralding the beginning of an unprecedented threat to the galaxy.

CHAPTER TWENTY-FOUR

Amidst the verdant splendor of Alan'dria, a scene of jubilation unfolded in the heart of the grand city. Towering spires adorned with vibrant foliage reached toward the cerulean sky, their graceful arcs a testament to the harmony between nature and civilization. Every Alan'drian is out in the main area of their city, their iridescent forms shimmering in the sunlight as they mingle with the other city dwellers, laughter echoing through the streets.

Every corner of the city is adorned with colorful banners and shimmering lights, casting a kaleidoscope of hues against the lush backdrop. The air hums with the melodious strains of music. Each note weaving a tapestry of joy and celebration. It is a day of triumph, a momentous occasion marking the election of a new leader, a beacon of hope and promise for the city and its inhabitants.

As the procession winds its way through the bustling streets, the leader, resplendent in regal attire, rides in a hovering vehicle, as a symbol of authority and grace. The cheers of the crowd mingle with the lilting laughter of children, their youthful exuberance adding to the infectious energy of the festivities. With every wave and smile, the new leader embodies the spirit of unity and progress, their presence a beacon of hope for a bright and prosperous future.

As the jubilant festivities reach their crescendo, an ominous disturbance ripples across the horizon, shattering the idyllic tranquility of Alan'dria. In an instant, the vibrant scene transforms into a tableau of disbelief and terror. A blinding flash of light pierces the sky, freezing the revelers in their tracks, as if time itself has ground to a halt.

A palpable chill descends upon the city, suffusing the air with a sense of foreboding. The once radiant sun dims ominously, casting a pall of darkness over the once jubilant streets. Gasps of horror echo through the crowd as debris from neighboring planets hurtle toward Alan'dria, raining destruction upon the unsuspecting city.

Panic seizes the hearts of the inhabitants, igniting a frenzy of chaos and terror. In the blink of an eye, the joyous celebration devolves into a scene of carnage and desperation. Frantic screams pierce the air, as people scramble for safety; their frantic attempts to escape only fueling the pandemonium.

Like a herd of panicked animals trapped within a kill zone, the throngs of people surge and jostle, each fighting for their survival amidst the chaos. The once vibrant streets become a battlefield of bodies, with desperation driving even the most peaceful of souls to acts of desperation.

Unbeknownst to the beleaguered inhabitants, Galgorn's sinister machinations has unleashed the unthinkable — the first test of his Solar Killer missile. From his vantage point, hidden away in the shadows, his menacing grin reflects off the monitor that bears witness to the devastation unfolding below. In that moment, the fate of Alan'dria is sealed, becoming a harbinger of the darkness threatening to engulf the entire galaxy.

Moments later, in a distant solar system, on the planet Prisalanti in the Ataritary System, a similar fate looms. Fifteen thousand light years away, Galgorn set his sights on a new target. The galaxy recoils as the malevolent orchestrator, fueled by a twisted desire for power, unleashes devastation on a planetary scale. As Galgorn watches with great pleasure he sends out a command, "Begin the next phase, I want to see how deadly the army is." A cold laughter, breaking into a mechanical sound, comes from Galgorn.

Above Prisalanti, an ominous fleet descends upon the unsuspecting world. The peacefulness that was once in the air, transforms into pandemonium as ships fire upon buildings and people, causing them to run and flee. Larger vessels materialize and land, disgorging a horde of cyborgs and pirates. The invaders pillage and loot with ruthless efficiency. Amidst the chaos, a lone pirate questions the senseless violence: "*I don't know what the point of all this is.*" Then, as quickly as the thought appears, apathy prevails.

"But who cares? I get a good pay day from all this." And the pillaging continues.

Galgorn's voice echoes across all communication frequencies on Prisalanti. A sinister announcement pierces the airwaves. "Good citizens of planet Prisalanti!" With a dark smile, one that can only come from a mind of pure vileness, he says, "I have no intentions of harming anyone, as long as you remain calm." The pirates stop pillaging, looking confused. Galgorn continues, "The more you panic, the more work in killing all of you we'll have to do." Every citizen screams as their fate is now sealed. "You're all nothing but a small step in testing out my machines…so on second thought…PANIC! Run! Hide! Give my creations a true test!"

As if on cue, people begin doing exactly as Galgorn commanded, as his intention to annihilate the entire population is made loud and clear. The planet responds with desperate resistance, deploying fighter crafts and ground troops to confront the invaders. However, their efforts falter, as the modified ships and relentless cyborgs prove nearly invincible. The invaders operate with complete precision, rendering the defenders virtually blind to their adversaries. One soldier yells out to another in frustration, "How can we fight these things? They appear and disappear! Even these damn infrared goggles don't work." It's the last words he utters before being impaled. All around the planet, panic-stricken people are fighting back as hard as they can, with futile results.

As Jalerg surveys the chaos unfolding below, from the vantage point of the ship, a twisted sense of satisfaction washes over him. Amidst the wreckage and carnage, he sees not just destruction, but opportunity. With a calculating gaze, he directs the cyborgs to scavenge the fallen, their lifeless bodies a grim resource for his macabre experiments.

"The spoils of war," Jalerg muses, his voice tinged with sinister amusement. "Fresh DNA samples, salvageable parts... all ripe for the taking." His mind whirls with possibilities, envisioning the creation of new enhanced cyborgs that will surpass anything seen before. "With these, we'll forge marvels," he declares, a malevolent grin twisting his features. "I'll transcend mere thievery and become a true master of creation."

As flames dance in his eyes, casting an eerie glow across his face, Jalerg's thoughts drift back to his tumultuous past. The memory of the cadet's murder lingers like a shadow, a reminder of his dark deeds. "I was a fugitive," he reflects, his tone laced with bitter irony, "but fate led me to Galgorn, and he saw beyond my crimes."

Glancing sidelong at Galgorn, a sense of unwavering loyalty surges within Jalerg. "He recognized my potential," he murmurs, his voice filled with reverence. "He offered me purpose, a chance to transcend my past and embrace a new destiny. For that, he has my undying devotion."

In the heart of the swirling chaos, Galgorn's twisted delight mirrors the devastation unfolding before him. With a smirk plastered across his face, he signals to Lyritha, urging her to prepare for their imminent departure. "Oh, come on," she protests, her voice laced with frustration. "It was just starting to get interesting; and think of the riches still ripe for the taking."

But Galgorn, unmoved by her pleas, insists on a more profitable endeavor lying in wait. "Stick to the plan," he reminds her, his words dripping with a chilling resolve. "Remember, your reward awaits you if you do." His icy gaze bore into the screen, sending shivers down Lyritha's spine, even from afar. "This is merely the initial phase, a precursor to the grand scheme. We must ensure every detail is flawless before we claim dominion over this universe. That's the essence of our endeavor," he declares harshly, punctuating his statement with a resounding fist against the table.

Though visibly unsettled, Lyritha quickly composes herself. "I know," she concedes, her tone betraying a hint of nervousness. "It's all about testing the efficiency of our forces."

Galgorn's nod of approval is accompanied by a steely gaze. "Precisely," he affirms. "Once we've identified any weaknesses and made the necessary adjustments, we'll be primed for the main event. Now, prepare yourself."

Despite her lingering hesitation, Lyritha complies, her resolve bolstered by the looming promise of glory. As Galgorn severs the communication, his grin widens, revealing the depths of his sinister intentions. "Foolish pirates," he mutters under his breath, his gaze narrowing with a chilling determination. "Little do they know what awaits them." With a side glance, he exchanges a confirming look with Jalerg, setting in motion the next phase of their malevolent scheme, each step inching them closer to their dark destiny.

As Galgorn prepares to resume his vigilant monitoring of the unfolding chaos, a stark silhouette of a figure appears on the screen, shrouding their identity in mystery. "Master," Galgorn intones reverently, bowing before the shadowy presence. "The testing progresses splendidly, and I am confident that once all is in readiness, your grand design shall be realized."

Acknowledging the progress made, the enigmatic figure urges Galgorn to maintain his unwavering dedication. "Do not falter, Galgorn," the voice resonates with an eerie authority. "You were crafted for a purpose beyond even the Doctor's comprehension."

With a chilling glare, the figure issues a dire warning, their words dripping with menace. "Should you fail me, rest assured, I will find alternative uses for your talents," they threaten, their tone brooking no dissent. The communication concludes abruptly, leaving Galgorn to contemplate the consequences of failure.

A sinister grin spreads across his face, his eyes gleaming with anticipation as he initiates the dawn of a new phase in his nefarious schemes. Across the galaxy, worlds will tremble in fear as the unholy alliance sets its sights on their next target, leaving only devastation and despair in its wake.

CHAPTER TWENTY-FIVE

In the cold expanse of space, the serenity of the cosmos is shattered by the unfolding of Galgorn's diabolical scheme. From the command center of his formidable flagship, Galgorn's augmented eyes gleam with a malevolent satisfaction, as he surveys the unfolding chaos below. The once-tranquil planet of Prisalanti, bathed in the soft glow of starlight, now trembles beneath the weight of impending doom.

With a gesture as smooth as the glide of a predator stalking its prey, Galgorn beckons forth the second fleet, their ominous silhouettes blotting out the stars as they advance with relentless purpose. "Let them witness the might of our armada." Galgorn's voice echoes with a chilling clarity through the bridge, his words laced with a twisted sense of amusement. "It's time to reveal our true power and leave no doubt as to who holds dominion over this galaxy." Galgorn lets out a menacing laugh, mixed with mechanical malice.

As the command reverberates through the ranks of his loyal followers, Galgorn's grin widens with an almost feral intensity. "Prepare to emerge from the shadows," he commands, his cybernetic hand dancing across the control panel with practiced precision. "Let them feel the weight of our presence and the full force of our wrath. There will be no mistaking the hand that guides their destruction."

With a burst of power, the flagship surges forward, its massive form emerging from the cloak of concealment with a deafening roar. As it looms menacingly in the void, its weapons primed and ready to unleash devastation upon the unsuspecting world below, Galgorn's laughter echoes through the void—a symphony of malevolence that heralds the dawn of a new era of darkness.

~~~~~~~~~~~~~

In the depths of space, in a distant solar system, bathed in the ethereal glow of a white dwarf star, a lone planet is nestled in the dark embrace of its hellish warmth. From the surface of this sinister sanctuary, countless ships begin to lift off, their sleek forms glinting ominously in the starlight. Above them all, Galgorn, the architect of chaos, watches with a sinister satisfaction, his eyes alight with the flames of conquest. From the shrouded cloak of night, the fleet assembles in silent anticipation, each ship a sleek silhouette against the backdrop of distant stars. At the heart of the armada, hidden by the shadow of a nearby moon, looms a behemoth—a colossal vessel, its sleek contours belying its formidable power.

With a command that reverberates through the cavernous depths of his flagship, Galgorn orders the activation of the Dimensional

Harmonic Drive (DHD2), a technology of unfathomable power capable of rending the fabric of space itself, and more advanced than its predecessor, the Dimensional Hop Drive. As the massive vessel hums with anticipation, a surge of energy erupts, tearing through the fabric of reality and birthing a colossal wormhole—a swirling maelstrom of cosmic energy, beckoning the armada forth into the unknown.

A twisted smirk graces Galgorn's lips as he beholds the gateway to oblivion, his eyes gleaming with malevolent glee. "It's time to sow the seeds of chaos," he declares, his voice a dark symphony of anticipation. "Let the universe tremble at the might of our wrath!" With a wicked laugh that echoes through the corridors of his flagship, Galgorn plunges headlong into the abyss, his thirst for destruction unquenchable.

In the heart of the bustling command center on Centima Four, Admiral Glark stands in front of the row of screens, his brow furrowed with concern as urgent reports flood in. The air crackles with tension as the gravity of the situation weighs heavily upon him, each transmission adding to the mounting sense of dread.

With a steely resolve, Admiral Glark's voice booms over the din, cutting through the chaos like a beacon of authority. "This is not a drill, repeat, not a drill! Prisalanti is under siege, and we are one of their last lines of defense. Prepare for immediate mobilization!" His orders echo off the walls, met with the swift hustle of crew members scrambling to their ships, their movements precise and purposeful.

Yet, amidst the flurry of activity, a palpable sense of foreboding grips the admiral's core, an ominous premonition gnawing at his subconscious like a persistent specter. As he surveys the frenzied scene before him, a shiver races down his spine, an eerie sensation akin to being ensnared in the plot of a nightmarish tale.

Suddenly, the air crackles with an otherworldly disturbance, a rippling rip in the fabric of space itself heralding the arrival of an unfathomable threat. With a sickening lurch, the command center shakes, as if recoiling from the impending doom. Admiral Glark's eyes widen in disbelief as the first shadowy silhouettes of Galgorn's armada materializes, their ominous presence casting a pall of despair over the defenders.

Before he can fully comprehend the magnitude of the danger, laser fire erupts with searing intensity, rending the once-sturdy walls of his bridge asunder. In a blur of chaos, the admiral finds himself engulfed by the deafening roar of destruction, the entire area reduces to a smoldering heap of rubble in the blink of an eye. Amidst the devastation, his cry of disbelief echoes, a poignant lament for the sudden and merciless onslaught that has befallen them.

Amidst the chaos, the defenders rally, their courage unwavering in the face of insurmountable odds. However, their valiant efforts are met with frustration as they struggle to target the elusive enemy ships. Jalerg's taunting laughter echoes through the chaos, a cruel reminder of their dire predicament.

In the dimly lit confines of the engineering bay, Jalerg's repeating laughter echoed off the metallic walls, a chilling symphony of malice. His grin, a twisted mask of satisfaction, betrays the depths of his depravity, as he surveys the chaos unfolding on the monitor before him.

With a self-satisfied smirk, Jalerg leans in closer to the display, his fingers dancing across the controls with a sinister grace. "Let them come," he murmurs, his voice dripping with venomous anticipation. "Our ships are but phantoms in the night, invisible to their feeble sensors. Thanks to my ingenuity and a few choice modifications, they're flying blind into our trap."

As the carnage unfolds onscreen, Jalerg's malevolent smile remains firmly in place, a silent testament to the success of his handiwork. His gaze locks on the flickering images before him and he revels in the chaos he has wrought, a puppet master pulling the strings of fate with ruthless precision.

Meanwhile, standing in the command deck, Galgorn's eyes gleam like a predator as he surveys the unfolding spectacle. With a subtle motion of approval, he acknowledges Jalerg's contribution to their nefarious scheme, a silent testament to the twisted partnership that bind them together in their quest for dominance. "Keep up the good work," he murmurs, his voice a low rumble of satisfaction. "I'll take it from here." With a purposeful stride, he turns and makes his way to the helm, his mind ablaze with visions of conquest and chaos.

Despite their training and determination, the defenders find themselves overwhelmed by the sheer ferocity of the onslaught. As the UPF regional headquarters burns and crumbles around them, they realize with growing horror that nothing could have prepared them for this nightmare. Their desperate struggle against an implacable foe seemed futile, their doom inevitable.

In the heart of the chaos, a beacon of resilience emerges as the rallying cry for aid echoes through the command center on Arigold. With steely determination, Admiral Sarklak marshals the scattered remnants of the defense forces, rallying them to stand firm against the tide of destruction sweeping across the galaxy.

"We've received distress signals from multiple fronts," he barks, his voice cutting through the din of battle with unwavering authority.

"Our comrades are under siege, and it's our duty to lend them our strength. All personnel, prepare to mobilize. We're heading to the front lines."

With a sense of urgency gripping their hearts, the crew on board the Olympus Starcruiser springs into action, their movements swift and purposeful as they prepare their ship for departure. Angelica, her resolve as unyielding as tempered steel, issues orders with a firm hand, her mind already racing to the challenges that lie in wait.

"Ensign P'thorkia, set course for Centima Four," she commands, her voice tinged with urgency. "We need to get there before it's too late. Galgorn's forces won't wait for us to catch up."

As the ship surges forward, cutting through the darkness of space with a determined fervor, Angelica can't shake the gnawing sense of apprehension that grips her heart. The fate of Centima Four hangs in the balance, and the weight of that responsibility bears down on her shoulders like a leaden burden.

But amidst the uncertainty and the looming threat of annihilation, there flickers a spark of hope—a glimmer of defiance that refuses to be extinguished. For as long as there are those willing to stand against the darkness, there will always be a chance for victory. And with each passing moment, the crew of the starship presses forward, their resolve unshakeable, their determination unwavering.

CHAPTER TWENTY-SIX

In the midst of chaos, reinforcements from the UPF surge into the fray around Centima Four, their arrival heralded by the thunderous roar of laser fire. The Olympus Starcruiser soars into the maelstrom, narrowly evading a barrage of hostile projectiles. "Damn it! That was close, I can't believe the carnage that's going on here," exclaims Angelica, holding onto her arm rest. With steely resolve, she surveys the unfolding chaos, her mind racing with strategies to counter the relentless assault as though this is nothing new to her. As she looks at her surroundings, she sees countless enemy ships pouring in and a disproportionate number of UPF ships either destroyed or completely inoperable. Without hesitation, she sends out her own fighter crafts into the chaos.

As each UPF vessel launches its defense crafts, they are met with fierce resistance from the enemy forces. Despite their valiant efforts, targeting the elusive enemy ships proves to be an exercise in futility. One by one, UPF ships fall under the relentless onslaught, their crews fighting desperately to repel the invaders. Angelica and the rest of the crew on board can't help but look at the carnage and think that the fighting will continue until the entire UPF fleet is distinguished.

Suddenly, the relentless barrage ceases, leaving a palpable tension hanging in the air. To the bewilderment of the UPF officers, the enemy ships begin to retreat, converging into the gaping maw of the still-open wormhole. Confusion ripples through the ranks, as they struggle to comprehend the sudden turn of events. Angelica looks on in wonders aloud, "What the hell is going on? Why would they retreat? Ensign Ta'yash, are you detecting anything?"

"No Captain!" Blarek responds quickly and continues scanning.

Then, a chilling voice resonates through the void, cutting through the silence like a knife. Somehow, all the ship's communication channels are taken over by a broadcast. It is Galgorn, the architect of this catastrophic assault, his words dripping with malice and contempt. "Greetings, officers of the UPF! You will all surrender today, and I might spare the remaining people. Refuse, and your days as protectors…" he lets out a mechanical laugh, "…will be over! You've seen what my forces can do. Make…your…choice!"

To underscore his threat, Galgorn unleashes a devastating salvo, from his cloaked flagship, toward the Olympus Starcruiser, crippling it with ruthless efficiency. Angelica's heart sinks as she braces herself, witnessing the devastation unfolding aboard her ship. Everyone onboard, her crew, her friends, fall victim to the merciless onslaught. The crew on the bridge of her ship brace themselves.

"Galgorn!" Angelica yells out angrily, as she stands up from her seat. She makes an announcement to the entire crew, "Hold steady everyone, we're not done yet! Not if we all still have breath in our lungs and blood in our veins. We will not faulter or..." She is interrupted as one of the consoles explodes behind her. She quickly continues, even in the face of such dire circumstances, proving that her spirit remains unbroken.

As Angelica grapples with the weight of Galgorn's ultimatum, a sense of dread washes over her. Galgorn makes another demand, "I also want Evander Guryon!" After a dramatic pause he continues, "I know what you must be asking. Why? Well, that's for me to know and for you all to keep on wondering."

The twisted tyrant seeks not only victory, but also the capture of Evander, Angelica's steadfast companion and friend. With grim determination, Angelica refuses to yield to Galgorn's demands. Her defiance unwavering in the face of overwhelming odds. She sends out a communication to Galgorn's ship. "We're not going to hand over Ensign Guryon to you! Do you understand that, you crazed son of a bitch?"

Galgorn responds, "So be it. I have ways of getting what I want from people. As for the rest of the UPF, they'll have you to thank for their downfall." Galgorn sends ships to recover the salvageable UPF fighter crafts. All the while, his face distorts into a face of extreme displeasure.

~~~~~~~~~~~~~

On a distant planet, bathed in the gentle glow of distant stars, Evander finds solace within the confines of his childhood home. Nestled within the familiar embrace of his family workshop, he toils away in quiet contemplation, his hands deftly guiding the intricate mechanisms of his faithful companion, Mal'Erro. The hum of machinery provided a soothing backdrop to his thoughts, a respite from the chaos that grips the cosmos beyond.

"There you go, give that a try," Evander says to Mal'Erro, who then turns into a can and then a ball. Evander is extremely happy with the progress. "Very good and how's your energy level? Is the new kinetic energy source working well for you?"

Mal'Erro whirs around and around, then stops and morphs back into a mini robotic humanoid form. "My power levels are at peak efficiency and the new kinetic energy source is working as intended. Thank you."

Evander is pleased to hear this and gives a gleeful smile in response. "That's excellent Mal'Erro. Now let's see about your defense capabilities, huh? Also, I want to see how your integrated camouflage unit is working." Evander checks Mal'Erro over as it mimics its surroundings, turning semi-invisible. "Oh, that's working like a charm. Might not be like the cloaking watch or core that those cyborgs had, but this should be the next best thing."

Mal'Erro gives out a whistle and rolls around. "Thank you, Evander. I hope the next upgrade is just as good."

Evander smiles with pleasure. His father's work and dreams for Mal'Erro is finally coming to fruition. Evander, who spent the last month and a half relaxing and slowly getting better, gives out a sigh of relief. He then pulls out a schematic of Mal'Erro and looks them over. The little robot comes next to him and, pointing at the schematic, asks "So what's this section about?"

Evander looks at Mal'Erro happily, as though the weight of the world has finally lifted off his shoulders. "This, my little friend, is going to be your next upgrade. This will give you the capability to merge with the ULTRA suit, enhancing its capabilities. It will also enhance yours as well."

Mal'Erro responds excitedly, "That sounds really great, Evander. I can't wait to finally be able to help out and assist in your duties." Mal'Erro then turns into a radio to play some music, but when it tunes into a station, Evander doesn't hear music—instead he hears the Galactic News.

The conflict that's currently going on reverberates through the airwaves and the tranquility of Evander's solitude is shattered by its intrusion. With rapt attention, he turns his gaze toward Mal'Erro and says, "Mal'Erro, turn that up." Mal'Erro complies. Evander listens intently, his heart heavy with apprehension as the dire tidings unfold before him. Amidst the tumult of battle, the name of Angelica's ship rings out like a clarion call. Its significance sending a shiver down his spine.

The news announcer continues, "…We've also got word that the being called Galgorn has demanded to see someone named Evander Guryon. Who is this person? What significance does he have with this monstrosity? We'll keep you all…"

Mal'Erro stops and turns back into a mini robot. With worry in its voice it asks, "Evander, do you think Angelica and the others are okay?"

In that moment, uncertainty grips Evander's heart, his mind awash with questions that linger like specters in the darkness. "I don't know Mal'Erro. Also, how many times do I have to tell you that you can just call me Evan?"

Mal'Erro just shrugs. Evander continues to think. What nefarious machinations lay behind Galgorn's insidious designs? And what role did fate have in store for him amidst the chaos that threatens to engulf them all?

With a resolve born of determination, Evander makes a fateful decision. His path set by the bonds of friendship and the call of duty that beckon him forth. Turning to his faithful companion, Mal'Erro, he speaks with solemn conviction; his words a solemn vow amidst the uncertainty that looms on the horizon. "Stay here, Mal'Erro," Evander murmurs, his voice tinged with a quiet resolution. "I'll return soon, but for now, you must remain here. Keep a watch on the house, my friend. I'll see you when I get back." With that, Evander starts to pack up his equipment.

Mal'Erro acknowledges Evander, it's metallic form standing sentinel amidst the confines of the workshop. As Evander makes his departure, the weight of the world heavy upon his shoulders, Mal'Erro watches in silent vigil. Its unwavering gaze follows Evander heading toward the shipyard, not knowing if Evander will return to this place.

Alone once more, Mal'Erro retreats into the cannister, its form disappearing from view as it nestles within the confines of its sanctum. With a quiet commitment, it awaited the return of its master, its metallic heart filled with hope amidst the uncertainty that looms on the horizon. The room goes silent, as though there was no one there.

Mal'Erro's cannister suddenly springs open. After reforming into a robot, it says aloud, "Hang on! Evand…Evan will most likely need assistance. I may not be able to combine with him yet, but I can still help him and the UPF." With gusto and determination, it decides to disobey Evander. It turns into a mini wheel with thrusters on the side. Using a burst of kinetic energy, Mal'Erro races to catch up to Evander. Just as the ship is about to launch, Mal'Erro gives everything it has and thrusts forward, attaching itself to the landing gear and molding its body around one of the legs. "That was close," Mal'Erro says as it prepares itself for the journey ahead. As it looks down, it sees how high up they are getting. This makes it soon realize that it is a little afraid of heights. "I'm sensing this might not have been the best idea. Please Evander, don't crash!" As the ship ascends, the landing gear retreats, with Mal'Erro hiding inside.

CHAPTER TWENTY-SEVEN

Back in the region of Centima Four, Angelica's ship finds itself ensnared by the relentless grip of Galgorn's flagship. Held captive within the heart of the enemy's armada, the crew stands on edge, their fate hanging in the balance, as they await Galgorn's next course of action. The tension is palpable, a silent battleground where neither side dares to make the first move.

As the stalemate persists, Galgorn's voice echoes through the void, breaking the silence with an order that sends ripples of anticipation through his ranks. "Get ready to attack on my command and decimate them all." Across the vast distances of space, the Pirate Queen Lyritha receives the call, her own ambitions aligned with Galgorn's insatiable thirst for conquest. With eager determination, she readies her forces for the impending onslaught, eager to claim her share of the spoils.

Aboard Galgorn's flagship, impatience gnaws at the tyrant's resolve. Tired of waiting for the inevitable, he issues the order to resume the assault. His hunger for domination driving him ever forward into the fray, he sends out the command, "Leave no one alive! If they don't want to surrender, then we'll wipe out the lot of them!" As the engines roar to life and the armada lurches into motion, the stage is set for a clash of titans, where the fate of worlds hangs in the balance.

As the cacophony of war reignites across the cosmic battlefield, Galgorn stands before the holo-screen, his eyes alight with a cold calculating gaze. With each flicker of light and burst of energy, he finds amusement in the futile efforts of the UPF ships, as they valiantly attempt to defend against his overwhelming forces. A sinister chuckle escapes Galgorn's lips, a chilling symphony of contempt and superiority. Despite the defiance of his adversaries, he remains steadfast in his conviction that victory is inevitable.

Jalerg, his dutiful lieutenant, watches on with a mixture of awe and uncertainty. As the battle unfolds before them, he cannot help but question the morality of their actions and the ultimate purpose of their conquest. Doubt gnaws at his fortitude, casting a pall of unease over his once unwavering loyalty.

Galgorn's keen gaze flickers toward Jalerg, detecting the subtle shift in his demeanor. With a knowing smirk, he recognizes the seed of doubt taking root within his lieutenant's mind. Yet, instead of addressing it, he chooses to revel in the chaos of war, confident in his own supremacy and the inevitability of his triumph. *"The fool will see; they will all see! This is all for the greater plan!"* Galgorn thinks to himself, with great assurance.

With a malevolent glint in his eyes, Galgorn issues a chilling command to Jalerg, his trusted subordinate. "Prepare the Solar Killer missiles," he declares, his voice dripping with malice and anticipation. Jalerg, ever obedient to his master's will, tilts his head solemnly in obedience and sets the wheels of destruction into motion. As the ominous hum of machinery fills the air, the Solar Killer missile is loaded into the sleek confines of the launch bay, its deadly payload primed and ready to unleash devastation upon the unsuspecting solar system. Galgorn watches with twisted delight as the missile ignites, a beacon of destruction hurtling toward its celestial target. "Let's see how defiant they are, when their solar system is no more!" With delight and a wide grin, Galgorn watches as the missile is launched at the sun. Even if attacked, he knows full-well the missile protected by a force field.

Yet, unbeknown to him, even as the missile hurtles through the void of space, a glimmer of hope emerges amidst the chaos. A vigilant UPF vessel, its sensors keen and its crew resolute, detects the telltale signs of impending doom. With lightning reflexes, they unleash a volley of laser fire in a desperate attempt to intercept the oncoming threat. However, despite their valiant efforts, the Solar Killer missile remains shrouded within an impenetrable shield, deflecting each salvo with contemptuous ease. With grim determination, the missile continues its inexorable advance toward the heart of the solar system, its thrusters primed to seal the fate of countless lives. In a few minutes, the missile will hit its target, like a perfectly thrown dart.

Amidst the chaos of battle, Evander's arrival in the system heralds a glimmer of hope for the beleaguered UPF forces. With nerves of steel, he maneuvers his ship through a maelstrom of laser fire, narrowly evading the deadly barrage of enemy attacks. From the corner of his eye, Evander spots a missile, not heading toward a ship, but toward the sun. *"Shit! I need to get to that missile, otherwise this entire system is lost."* Evander valiantly heads toward it.

He gets a communications relay from one of the ships that attempted to take it down. "Evander, why the hell are you here? Know what? Doesn't matter. I wouldn't bother firing at it. It's protected by a force field. Unless you got an EMP cannon on that ship, we're screwed!" The UPF officer ends the transmission.

As he prepares to try and figure out a way around the defenses of the missile and to join the fray with the others, Evander is startled by a sudden tug at his leg. "What the hell...?" Startled, he glances downward to find Mal'Erro, his mischievous robotic companion, vying for his attention. "What in the hell are you doing here? O, great, I sound like that UPF officer." Evander takes a deep breath and says, "Obviously I can't take you back, so just stay out of trouble, while I try and get us both back in one piece, alright?"

Though initially annoyed by the interruption, Evander quickly refocuses his attention on the urgent matter at hand. A moment later he hits his arm rest and says angrily, "Damn it, I can't think of what to do! How in the world am I going to take down that force field? I only have a few minutes left! I suppose I could just ram it."

With a sense of urgency, Mal'Erro offers, "Might I offer a suggestion? Why not modify one of the cannons to emit an EM pulse toward the missile? That should disable it long enough to destroy it."

Despite the inherent risks, Evander recognizes the potential efficacy of Mal'Erro's plan. Modulating the ship's lasers to emit a magnetic pulse sounds possible. Evander agrees and tells Mal'Erro to go and make the lasers capable of disrupting the shield's defenses.

Meanwhile, two enemy ships spot Evander pursuing the missile and change course to intercept. As Evander looks back up, he spots a shimmer, which he finds odd and out of place. Without hesitation, he fires and immediately sees sparks. The UPF officer in the other ship sees it too and they simultaneously realize that, though the enemy ships are invisible, if a light source is powerful enough, the invisibility will cause a shimmering effect. With nerves of steel, they engage the enemy with unmatched skill and determination, evading each incoming laser blast with fearless agility. Together they manage to take out two enemy ships.

"How's it coming with those modifications Mal'Erro? I don't know how long me and the other officer can hold out with these guys, even with our little trick." Mal'Erro plays a siren sound to give the go ahead. "Excellent!" Evander reopens communications with the other UPF craft and tells him to get ready to fire at will.

As the crucial moment arrives, Evander fires the modified cannon and hits the missile. The shield surrounding the Solar Killer missile falters, leaving it vulnerable to a decisive strike from both his ship and the UPF fighter craft. They unleash a devastating barrage of laser fire, their aim true and their perseverance unyielding. With a resounding explosion and a sense of triumph, both Evander and the other officer watch as the missile is obliterated. Its deadly payload neutralized before it can wreak havoc upon the solar system, with mere moments to spare.

As the other officer heads back to the main battle after offering his thanks, Evander's moment of victory is short-lived when grim news reaches his ears. The Olympus Starcruiser and its crew, including Angelica, have fallen into the clutches of the malevolent Galgorn. A chill runs down Evander's spine as he realizes the true cost of their defiance, his own capture at the hands of the enemy. "If Galgorn wants me, then that's what he'll get. Mal'Erro, I need you to go and hide somewhere safe. If Galgorn gets his hands on you, who knows what he might do." Mal'Erro obeys and hides, while Evander makes his way toward the giant flagship.

~~~~~~~~~~~~~

Fury consumes Galgorn as he strikes the console with a resounding blow, the impact echoing through the command bridge. Startled, Jalerg recoils in fear, his eyes wide with apprehension, as he witnesses the dark storm brewing within their leader. With a steely gaze, Galgorn commands Jalerg to ready a new missile for immediate launch, his voice dripping with menace and impatience.

Jalerg hesitates, and says, "I'm sorry sir, but the other missile isn't ready yet. I was only able to make three, but the third one was having some issues. You already used the first two, but I'll get to work on it and ready the launch. I just need an hour, an hour and a half max!"

This response brings a scowl to Galgorn's face, frustration mounting with each passing moment. Despite Jalerg's assurances of swift preparation, Galgorn's impatience knows no bounds. With a growl of exasperation, he begrudgingly accedes to the delay, though his wrath simmers beneath the surface like a dormant volcano on the verge of eruption.

Leaving the bridge in a whirlwind of anger, Galgorn stalks toward the holding cells with purposeful strides, his mind consumed by thoughts of retribution. He approaches Angelica and her imprisoned crew. His voice drips with venom as he delivers the chilling news of Evander's interference and its consequences.

Angelica yells out, "Evander's here? Good! We're glad he was able to destroy that missile of yours."

Galgorn is unphased by her reaction. He informs her that, if that makes her happy, what will it take to make her unhappy? Besides the obvious, he wants to know what will truly break her like a mirror broken by a hammer. "Let's do some experimentation, shall we? Let's see how much pain one or more of your crew members can take! I need to take out my frustrations on someone," Galgorn tells Angelica with disdain and malice. "That one seems like a good candidate," he says, pointing at one of Calidorfian engineers.

Angelica pleads with him and Lieutenant Commander Froslo starts swearing and cursing like he's never done before. Ignoring them, Galgorn gives an order to one of his cyborgs and the selected Calidorfian is dragged out of the cell, kicking and screaming so loud that a banshee would be afraid. Moment's later, everyone in the cell could hear the Calidorfian scream in anguish.

With a heavy heart, Jalerg watches from the shadows, as he observes the Calidorfian being tortured. His doubts are gnawing at his conscience like insidious whispers. Though he is a murderer himself, even he has a line that he will not dare cross. As the weight of his allegiance to Galgorn hangs heavy upon him, he begins to question the path he has chosen, uncertain of the darkness that lies ahead.

CHAPTER TWENTY-EIGHT

As Evander is heading toward the Galgorn's flagship, he gets a communications request. A flicker of relief washes over him as the communication from Admiral Sarklak crackles to life. His heart races with anticipation as he awaits the admiral's words. "Ensign Guryon, what in the hell are you doing there? I thought you were put on mandatory leave?"

Evander takes a deep breath, and while still dodging weapons fire, says, "Yes sir, technically I am, but I can't stand idly by when the UPF and another world is burning. And the demands made were Galgorn wanting me… and the surrender of the UPF."

"I don't care Evander, you shouldn't be there. I don't know what makes you so damn special that Galgorn wants you, but you need to turn around."

For the first time since Evander has known him, the admiral sounds afraid. Unshaken, and with conviction and determination in his voice, he responds, "Sir, with all due respect, I'm going to disobey that. I'm still a UPF officer and though I shouldn't be here, I am now, and I will help and do my duty!"

The admiral is taken aback by this. "Ensign Guryon… Evander, I'll be real with you right now. I don't want to see you end up dead.

You hear me?" With a somber tone he says, "I promised your parents I would try my very best to ensure nothing bad happens to you. Or at the very least you are well prepared to being able to handle yourself." The admiral makes great effort to hold the tears forming. "If you die, I would have failed that promise and I'm not sure you are even ready yet, despite the number of missions you have done. Each one of those missions, I hate to admit, were hand picked."

Evander is shocked at the news. While still fighting his way through a swath of enemy ships, dodging laser fire, he asks, "Sir, if you didn't think I was ready, why did you allow me to graduate? Why let me even go on those missions?" Evander takes a deep breath in. "I hate to do this, but I must disagree with you. I am ready, and though I'm not good with a sword, I know I can take care of myself." He looks down over at Mal'Erro. "Thanks to you, even though you were harsh with us, I learned a lot of valuable lessons. I reflected a lot during my time away and one thing I must say is… Shit!"

The admiral responds, confused, "What was that? I wasn't expecting that response."

Evander quickly responds, "Sorry sir. That's not what I wanted to say. I nearly got hit by a stray laser fire from one of our own. Anyways, I just wanted to say… Next to my mother and father, I do look up to you. That's why I will try my hardest not to let you or anyone else down. One of the lessons you taught me was, as a UPF officer, no matter what, we must always be vigilant, respectful and to always be a protector, even when things look tough!"

With genuine admiration in his voice the admiral concedes, "I guess even I need a reminder from time to time. You have certainly grown Evander. Your parents would both be proud of you." As Admiral Sarklak commends Evander for his valiant efforts in thwarting the deadly missile threat, his words balm Evander's weary soul.

Yet, amidst the accolades, Admiral Sarklak's stern tone comes back and carries a weighty reminder of duty and obligation. "Evander, since you're determined to stay and help fight, I cannot stop you. But if we survive this, promise me one thing." The admiral waits for Evander's agreement, then continues, with a gentle, but firm, demeanor, "I want to impress upon you Evander the importance of honoring your remaining leave and emphasize the necessity of rest and recuperation, even in the face of this impending danger. Now do what you must and kick these bastard's asses back to where they came from."

Mal'Erro cheers enthusiastically, and the admiral, upon hearing it in the background says, "And may I suggest keeping…Mal'Erro out of the battle next time." Despite the gravity of the situation, Admiral Sarklak's unwavering tenacity shines through. His confidence in Evander's abilities serves as a beacon of hope amidst the encroaching darkness. With a final warning of the dire stakes at hand, he bids Evander farewell, his words echoing with the urgency of their perilous predicament.

A chill sweeps through the air, as Galgorn's voice cuts through the static of the communication channel, his ominous presence casting a shadow over the fleeting moment of respite. "I was wondering when you two would end your communication. Didn't want to interrupt. I have your comrades Evander. If you want to see most of them still, you will come to my ship. I'll even make it easy for you and have my troops not attack you. If not, I'll just kill the rest of your fellow officers and let Jalerg use their remains as spare parts for his experiments." Galgorn's words drip with malice and deceit. Like a spider weaving its web, he spins a web of deception, offering a false promise of amnesty in exchange for surrender.

Despite the discernible danger lurking beneath Galgorn's honeyed words, Evander's strength of will remains unbroken, his keen intuition alerting him to the treacherous trap laid before him. With a steady voice, he acquiesces to Galgorn's demands, his mind already racing with plans to outwit the cunning tyrant. Evander halts his ship and replies, "Fine, but I want you to release my fellow officers, unharmed! Agree to this and I'll come quietly." Even in the face of imminent peril, Evander refuses to abandon his principles, his unwavering loyalty to his comrades driving him to negotiate for their freedom. With a steely gaze, he confronts Galgorn.

In a chilling twist of fate, Galgorn begrudgingly accedes to Evander's request, his begrudging acquiescence masking a deeper, more insidious agenda. "Very well, see you soon…brother."

As Evander prepares to embark on his perilous journey into the lion's den, he knows that the path ahead is fraught with danger and uncertainty. Yet, guided by his unwavering sense of duty and determination, he braces himself for the trials that lie ahead, his spirit unyielding in the face of darkness. As he heads toward Galgorn's ship, he glances over at Mal'Erro and in a hushed tone, says, "You better go hide. I'm not sure if Galgorn heard you or not, but still, best hide just in case." Mal'Erro agrees and quickly goes and hides.

As Evander reaches the ship, he is welcomed into the loading bay. A wave of horror washes over Evander as he steps onto the cold, metallic surface of Galgorn's flagship, his heart heavy with the weight of despair. "I'm here, now release my comrades," Evander yells out.

"Very well, a deal's a deal, right?" Galgorn's voice comes over the ship's communication. He tells his cyborgs, in a low tonal voice, to let Angelica's ship go and to hold Evander. Moments later Evander sees the ship undock and begin to leave, thinking that they're safe now. Galgorn screams over the communications system in a swift and cold demand, "Now fire!" and his ship fires at Angelica's ship, obliterating it.

With trembling hands, Evander watches in disbelief, as the silhouette of the Olympus Starcruiser fades into the distance, its once-proud form reduced to nothing more than a smoldering wreck. The bitter taste of betrayal lingers on Evander's tongue as Galgorn's callous laughter echoes through the cavernous expanse of the docking bay. In that moment of cruel realization, Evander's world shatters around him, his hopes dashed upon the jagged rocks of betrayal and deceit. With a defiant cry of anguish, Evander unleashes his fury upon the uncaring void, his voice a primal howl of despair that reverberates through the corridors of the flagship. Yet, even as he grapples with the crushing weight of loss, Galgorn's twisted words claw at the fringes of his mind, a venomous whisper that seeks to poison his endurance.

The interior ship door into the loading bay opens, and through it, Galgorn emerges in all his cybernetic glory, wearing a modified version of the ULTRA suit. Beneath the veneer of Galgorn's deceit lies a glimmer of truth, a flickering ember of defiance that refuses to be extinguished.

With a steely gaze, Evander confronts the tyrant before him, his spirit unbroken by the cruel machinations of fate. "You bastard! We had a deal!" In the face of overwhelming adversity, he stands resolute, his determination burning bright amidst the encroaching darkness.

"Yes, we did, and I held it. I said I would let them go, as soon as you got here. You just didn't specify how long I had to wait before I could get rid of them." Galgorn laughs and instructs a few of his cyborgs to take Evander and bring him to the bridge. As Evander is roughly seized by the cold, unyielding grasp of the cyborgs, a sense of helplessness washes over him like a tide of despair. Tears mingle with the anger that simmers beneath the surface, his heart heavy with the weight of loss. Yet, even as he is dragged toward an uncertain fate, a flicker of hope remains, a defiant spark that refuses to be extinguished.

Mal'Erro slithers out of Evander's ship and quickly scans the area around him. Seeing that the coast is clear, it camouflages with the floor and slithers its way toward a door. Amidst the shadows of the flagship's labyrinthine corridors, Mal'Erro moves with silent precision, its form shrouded in the cloak of almost invisibility. With each calculated step, it navigates the treacherous terrain, its senses keenly attuned to the slightest whisper of danger. It then sees some cyborgs approaching, so it stops and hides in the corner, hoping not to be seen. After they're gone, it goes back on the move again.

Suddenly, a familiar sound catches Mal'Erro's attention, a faint echo that reverberates through the darkness like a beacon in the night. With care and stealth, it follows the elusive trail, silently reverberating with anticipation as it draws ever closer to the source of the noise.

In the dimly lit confines of the holding cells, amidst the despair that hangs heavy in the air, the lies of Galgorn are revealed. Angelica is huddled alongside Kal'korg, Blarek, Froslo, P'thorkia, and the rest of the remaining crew. Despite the dire circumstances, they cling to each other, their spirits unbroken even in the face of adversity.

In this moment of reprieve Kal'korg offers solace to Blarek, his comforting words a beacon of light in the darkness. "I swear, we'll be all right. I'm sure the UPF are finding a way to defeat Galgorn and are coming to rescue us." Blarek hugs Kal'korg tightly. Nearby, Froslo and the other Calidorfian's colorful vocabulary fills the air, a testament to his resilience in the face of danger. Yet, amidst the cacophony of emotions, Angelica remains silent in a corner, her expression a mask of sorrow and dread.

Just as despair threatens to consume her, a curious sound reverberates from within the walls, capturing Angelica's attention.

"What in the world? Now what? What is Galgorn planning on doing now to us?" Intrigued, she cautiously approaches the source of the noise, her companions watching with bated breath. With P'thorkia's assistance, Angelica investigates a vent, unaware of the surprise awaiting them. "The noise seems to be coming from inside here. What is it?"

P'thorkia puts her hand on Angelica's shoulders. "I'll check it out." Angelica watches nervously from the side as P'thorkia reaches out to touch the vent. Suddenly, a metallic type of goo substance latches onto her face, muffling her startled cry. Everyone in the cell is taken aback and frozen with shock, until a robot head emerges from the goo, its presence both unexpected and welcome.

Relief washes over Angelica as she recognizes Mal'Erro, its unexpected arrival sparking a glimmer of hope within her heart. "Mal'Erro, how did you get here? Wait, is Evander here?" Angelica's heart sinks.

Mal'Erro nods its head enthusiastically and explains, "Evander traded himself for your lives, but when he came here, Galgorn betrayed him and destroyed your ship. He made Evander believe you were all on it and are now dead."

P'thorkia taps Mal'Erro, which causes it to realize that it is still on her face. It leaps off her and onto the floor. "He will be most pleased that you're still alive. He's still in a fragile state, even though he has gotten much better. Or at least he was. But once he sees you, he should be back to the state he was before."

Angelica stops Mal'Erro. "You said he came here to give himself up to save us. Did you hear where they've taken him?"

Mal'Erro responds, "Yes. Galgorn took him to the bridge."

Angelica thinks for a moment and forms a plan. "Mal'Erro how wide are those vents? And how much weight can you hold?" Everyone, including Mal'Erro, looks at her in confusion. With Mal'Erro's aid, Angelica hatches a daring plan to escape their captivity, her determination unyielding. Together, they stand ready to defy their captors and reclaim their freedom. Their bond, forged in the crucible of adversity, stronger than ever before.

CHAPTER TWENTY-NINE

The tension aboard Galgorn's flagship is discernible, as distant screams echo through the corridors. Outside, the battle rages on relentlessly, leaving a trail of debris in its wake. Amidst the chaos, the vast armada of the UPF appear to be losing ground, their ships dwindling against the onslaught of Galgorn's forces. However, hope emerges on the horizon as new wormholes begin to open, heralding the arrival of reinforcements. With each new arrival, the UPF fleet grows stronger, launching a defiant counterattack against Galgorn's armada.

Yet, on the bridge of the flagship, Jalerg remains composed, his gaze fixed on the holo-screen before him. Despite the appearance of adversity, he exudes an air of confidence, assured that the advanced ships, crafted by himself and Galgorn, will swiftly dispatch the incoming threats.

Bound to a chair on the command deck of Galgorn's flagship, Evander strains against his restraints, his muscles taut with effort as he attempts to free himself. Each futile struggle only serves to deepen the sense of despair gnawing at his soul. Emotions churn within him, a tumultuous storm raging beneath the surface. The month of respite he has just completed feels like a fleeting memory, overshadowed by the grim reality of his captivity. Thoughts of his friends and comrades, lost in the chaos of battle, weighs heavily upon him, threatening to shatter his fortitude.

Yet, amidst the turmoil, a flicker of determination burns within Evander's heart. Despite the overwhelming odds stacked against him, he refuses to yield to despair. With gritted teeth and clenched fists, he vows to find a way to break free from his captivity and halt the relentless onslaught threatening the galaxy.

As Galgorn's mocking words cut through the air, Evander strains against his bonds, his frustration evident. "Galgorn, I still don't understand, what the hell do you want with me?" he demands, his voice edged with defiance.

Galgorn circles around him with a sinister smirk, his presence exuding an aura of malevolence. "Oh, you have a great purpose to fulfill," he replies cryptically, his tone dripping with contempt. "You see, while I was wandering around after escaping, I stumbled upon something rather intriguing—a cave, a cave like no other."

Leaning in close, Galgorn's eyes gleam with a twisted delight. "Inside, I saw ancient writings. It took me a while to decipher," he continues, relishing the moment. "Finally, though, I was able to read what it said. It was a prophecy, a tale of cosmic proportions. But more importantly, it spoke of a piece of ancient technology that could reshape the universe."

Evander's confusion deepens, his brow furrowing in bewilderment. "What do I have to do with anything though?" he demands again, his voice tinged with frustration.

Galgorn's grin widens, reveling in Evander's uncertainty. "Everything!" he declares triumphantly. "The prophecy spoke of two brothers and a war—a war with the entire universe. One brother, a golem forged from earth and steel, and the other, a being made of stars."

With a sudden realization dawning upon him, Evander's eyes widen in shock. "You're the golem," he murmurs, the pieces of the puzzle falling into place. "And I'm the one made of stars?"

Galgorn's laughter echoes through the chamber, a chilling sound that sends shivers down Evander's spine. "Precisely," he confirms, his tone laced with malice. "And now, my dear brother, the time has come for us to play our roles in this cosmic drama."

With a twisted sense of satisfaction, Galgorn directs Evander's gaze toward the immense holo-screen dominating the bridge. The playback reveals the devastating aftermath wrought by the Solar Killer missile; its destructive power laid bare for all to witness. As the scenes unfold, "It took me and Jalerg a while to reverse engineer these missiles. Even with our combined knowledge. Lesson we learned, we should have stolen the plans, as well. But eventually, we were able to recreate the technology." Galgorn's voice drips with malevolent pride, as he recounts the meticulous process of reverse engineering the deadly weapon.

With a chilling calmness, Galgorn continues, "Of course, we needed to make some modifications. We aren't in the business of surveying stars after all." He goes on to explain the sinister purpose behind the Solar Killer missiles, detailing how they have been transformed into instruments of annihilation, capable of unraveling the very fabric of star systems. He speaks of Jalerg's painstaking efforts to recreate the intricate plans, their ultimate goal being the destabilization and destruction of stars, triggering catastrophic collapse.

Fueled by a mixture of anger and disbelief, Evander demands to know the rationale behind such wanton destruction. "Why are you doing this, though? What exactly do you hope to achieve from this?" His voice trembles with barely contained fury, as he questions the madness driving Galgorn's relentless pursuit of chaos and devastation.

In response, Galgorn's retort cuts through the air like a dagger, a sinister grin playing upon his lips, as he reveals the chilling truth behind his actions. "Because it's what I was programmed to do. And before you ask, no it wasn't your father that programmed me, and who did is my secret."

As the weight of Galgorn's revelation settles upon him, Evander's complexion pales, a shiver coursing down his spine at the implications of his adversary's words. The realization that such malevolence could be ingrained within the very core of Galgorn's being sends a cold chill through his veins. Yet, before he can dwell further on the implications, Galgorn says, "Oh, there's no need to worry about such things, big brother. Everything will be revealed in time." Galgorn's ominous warning shatters his train of thought, leaving him to grapple with the unsettling truth lurking beneath the surface.

In a desperate struggle for survival, Evander finds himself ensnared in Galgorn's merciless grip, a bio-mechanical hand fastened securely around his neck and the pressure on his throat tightening with each passing moment. Gasping for air, his vision blurs as Galgorn's taunting words echo in his ears. "I could snap your neck, just like I did Father's." Yet, even as darkness threatens to consume him, Evander summons every ounce of strength within him, refusing to succumb to the same fate that has befallen their father.

With a savage ferocity, Galgorn reaches for a blade, his intentions clear, as he seeks to end Evander's life with cold, ruthless efficiency. "I doubt I need you alive for the prophecy to be fulfilled. I'm thinking it has something to do with your DNA, and if that's the case, I just need your blood."

Fate intervenes in the form of a well-aimed shot, shattering the tension-laden silence, as Angelica emerges from the shadows, her presence a beacon of hope amidst the chaos. In a flurry of movement, the tide of battle shifts as Angelica and her loyal comrades reveal themselves, their steadfastness unwavering in the face of adversity.

"Evander, how many times do we have to save your ass!" Blarek remarks with a nervous laugh, as he watches Galgorn's head turn toward them.

Galgorn's fury reaches its crescendo, and he shouts, "You stupid freaking bitch! I should have just killed you in that torture chamber!" He launches himself at Angelica with savage intent, only to be thwarted by the timely intervention of Blarek, whose swift action sends Galgorn crashing to the ground.

Blarek steadies himself, and with vigor, says, "You should have paid closer attention!"

Seizing the opportunity, Mal'Erro maneuvers through the chaos, its stealthy approach enabling it to free Evander from his restraints. "Thanks buddy, although, remind me later to talk to you about listening. For now, I'm just glad you didn't and are here now." Looking quickly around he asks, "Hey, do you think you can get control of the ship?"

Mal'Erro confirms. "Yes! I just need to get to the controls and integrate with them. If you can keep the ugly one over there occupied long enough, I can."

With their adversary momentarily occupied, Angelica and her comrades rally together, their unity a testament to their unwavering and unyielding spirit. In a bold display of defiance, they unleash a coordinated assault, each blow striking true as they fight to claim control of the ship. In a final act of defiance, Angelica and Blarek deliver a decisive blow, sending Galgorn hurtling out of the command deck and into the corridor. With Galgorn's attention diverted, he doesn't see Mal'Erro seizing control of the ship's systems. The little robot locks the doors to the bridge to prevent further intrusion before Galgorn can get back inside.

Galgorn and the other cyborgs pound on the door with their fists, their frustration echoing through the chamber. Ignoring them, Evander quickly hugs Angelica, who hugs him back and hands him a pistol. Evander tucks away the weapon and turns to Mal'Erro and Angelica, seeking a solution amidst the chaos. "The UPF won't last too much longer out there. Galgorn's army just keeps coming. There has to be a way to stop them." He proposes the idea of creating a feedback loop to disrupt the cyborgs.

Mal'Erro confirms that Evander's plan can work for the other cyborgs, both on the flagship and the accompanying ships. However, it notes, "Just so you know, Galgorn is disconnected from the ship's systems. He would remain unaffected, along with any others not in the immediate vicinity. I also should point out, that the ship won't be able to respond to any commands either." He warns them that, while they can implement the feedback loop for the cyborgs within the ship, they will not be able to prevent reinforcements from arriving.

Evander pats Mal'Erro on the shoulders. "Then we better find a way to also get rid of Galgorn and stop his army from the source." Another idea suddenly pops into his head, and he says, "Galgorn mentioned another missile onboard. What if we used that? We aim it back into the worm hole and into that system's star. Could we do it?" But before anyone can answer, Evander has a moment of clarity. He realizes the significance of the flagship as the anchor point for the wormhole, connecting it to Galgorn's main base on the other side. He says, excitedly, "Wait, is this ship acting as an anchor? I just realized the wormhole didn't close."

Mal'Erro thinks quickly. "Yes, this ship is also the anchor for the wormhole. We would need to destroy it before the shockwave comes through. With the wormhole facing toward the planet, it would be like a giant death beam." Mal'Erro goes back to thinking, "But that means we might need to hold off on the feedback loop."

Angelica chimes in, "Send the ship through with it. Set it so the missile is launched just as the ship goes through. Also, having it self-destruct just after launch, would that work? Even if we don't do a feedback loop, any remaining forces out there won't be that hard to take care of."

As Mal'Erro thinks it over, Lieutenant Commander Froslo is getting frustrated waiting. "Would you make a decision, already? I don't know how long that door will hold, and I don't even want to think about our forces out there."

"Fine," Angelica responds quickly. "Mal'Erro, make it happen." Determined, she instructs Mal'Erro to alter the ship's course. Then she takes a moment and turns to her lead engineer and says, "Hey Froslo, that's the first time I didn't hear you swear. Did you decide to give it up?"

Froslo looks at her and, with great conviction, replies "No freaking bloody way in tarnation!"

Angelica rolls her eyes and replies, "Thought as much."

CHAPTER THIRTY

On the other side of the door, Galgorn taunts them with his laughter, relishing in their dilemma. "You won't be able to escape from here and you know it." After not hearing a response, Galgorn's fury is fueled even more, and he starts pounding on the door with increasing intensity.

As he's pounding, he hears his personal communicator going off. When he answers, he hears Jalerg's voice crackling over his communicator, informing Galgorn that the missile was primed for launch. Impatient, and seething with anger, Galgorn demands immediate action. "Put the missile into the launcher already then, damn it! And fire it!"

"All right," Jalerg replies. "But the loading process will take some time without the help of any cyborgs." Galgorn looks around and realizes that all cyborgs are currently stationed next to him outside the command deck. Frustrated by the delay, Galgorn begrudgingly accepts the explanation, urging Jalerg to expedite the process.

Meanwhile, Evander's keen eye catches a flashing light on the console, signaling activity in the launching bay. "Looks like we've got a wrench in our plans folks." Evander points to the screen, as he sees Jalerg tinkering with the missile. Sensing an opportunity, he turns to Mal'Erro and asks, "Is there a way down there from here, without opening that door?"

Mal'Erro looks around in the database, seeking a way to reach the bay swiftly. Mal'Erro confirms that a route exists through the ducts, albeit a cramped one.

"That will have to do," Evander affirms. "Route the path to my UI and I'll head down there. Hopefully before Jalerg finishes whatever it is he's doing." Without hesitation, Evander embarks on the perilous journey, knowing that time is of the essence.

As Evander departs, Galgorn's attention is drawn to his movements. "I hear someone opening one of the ducts." Galgorn quickly goes through the schematics on his own personal database and exclaims, "Someone is heading toward the launching bay!" He orders his cyborgs to intensify their efforts to breach the door, while he goes and intercepts whomever it is that's going to the launching bay. The tension in the air grows palpable as both sides race against the clock, each with their own objectives and strategies in play.

In the launching bay, tension hangs heavy in the air. Evander jumps down from the ventilation duct and immediately confronts Jalerg. Determined to hold him accountable for his crimes, he says, "Jalerg! You are under arrest, by the authority of the Universal

Peacekeeping Federation! Stop what you are doing and come with me."

Jalerg's laughter echoes off the metal walls, a chilling counterpoint to Evander's accusations. "Who and what army? Yours is dwindling, while ours keeps growing! And once this star is destroyed, you'll be made even weaker."

With grim determination, Evander levels his accusations. But Jalerg dismisses them with a casual wave of his hand, his amusement evident. "You're boring me," Jalerg says with a smirk and a laugh. "I remember you from training, I'm surprised you even passed!"

As Jalerg reaches for the launch button, Evander's reflexes kick into action. He pulls out his pistol, like a viper striking with extreme accuracy, his shot shattering the console in a burst of sparks. Yet, Jalerg's reaction is not one of shock, but rather a sardonic grin, as he reveals the fail-safes built into the system. "Thanks, now the missile is just going to fire anyways," Jalerg says, laughing and planting his hands firmly on the console. "Just not at the planet below, but one of your own ships! Either way it's going to destroy something."

Evander's heart sinks at the realization that their efforts might have been in vain. However, his determination remains unbroken, as he asserts control over launch bay. "That maybe true, but I think my fellow officers can find a way." While still pointing his weapon at

Jalerg, Evander contacts Angelica. "Hey, we've got an issue here. The missile was primed and ready to go before I got here, but the console was smashed before the missile's destination was set."

Mal'Erro confirms, but gives hopeful news, "That's okay, just keep whoever is down there busy. I think I can redirect and buy us some time from up here."

"Thanks buddy!" Evander says and directs his focus back to Jalerg. He begins to move toward him to put on restraints, but a sudden blow from behind sends Evander crashing to the ground.

Galgorn looms over his fallen foe, his eyes gleaming with malice. "You stupid bastard! You just had to come down here and interfere, didn't you?"

In the heat of battle, chaos reigns supreme as Jalerg seizes the opportunity to slip away unnoticed, leaving Galgorn and Evander locked in a fierce struggle. Galgorn, revealing his upgraded capabilities, vanishes from sight, leaving Evander to face an unseeable adversary. "What do you think of my newest upgrade Evander? It's one of many! Let's see if you can live long enough to see the other ones." Galgorn starts attacking, Evander unable to see, gets tossed around as easily as a ragdoll.

Evander keeps trying to evade, but to no avail. Galgorn keeps knocking him around, while Evander tries to think of what to do. Sensing the extreme danger he's in, Evander activates his helmet's space mode feature. As he readies himself for the confrontation, he says, "I've prepared for this as well, Galgorn!" With calculated precision, he deploys a specialized grenade, releasing a cloud of bioluminescent particles into the air. Shielded by his helmet's advanced filtration system, Evander remains unaffected as the particles illuminate the invisible foe, revealing Galgorn's presence. "There you are!" Evan exclaims. Galgorn growls like a cornered mad lion.

Armed with newfound visibility, Evander deftly avoids Galgorn's attacks, capitalizing on the tyrant's mounting frustration and increasing propensity for errors. "What's wrong Galgorn? Thought you were supposed to be better than most officers of the UPF? What about those other upgrades you mentioned?"

Galgorn stops his assault. "You want to see the other upgrades I gave myself? Very well." Galgorn then presses a button on his wrist, and from his sides, two other arms appear, one with a portable force field that acts like a shield. Evander looks on in horror, wondering what he's going to do now!

Amidst the chaos, Mal'Erro relays to Evander that it's ready for the next step in their daring plan. As Evander continues to dance through Galgorn's strikes, and is finally given a window of opportunity, he gives his assent to Mal'Erro. This serves as the instruction for it to set the course and prepare for a coordinated strike that can turn the tide of the battle.

In a moment of fury, Galgorn's rage proves to be his undoing as he loses his balance and stumbles onto the missile, one of his arms getting lodged underneath. Seizing the opportunity, Evander acts swiftly. "This is for Father and Kes!" He severs Galgorn's head from his body and as Galgorn's body lays lifeless over the missile, his head rolls on the floor. Evander picks it up and then quickly secures it to the missile's rear.

Despite his grim fate, Galgorn's laughter echoes through the chamber, his ominous words lingering in the air, "If you think, fo...r a moment..." he begins to fizzle and stutter, "this... this is the end, you are...sore...sorely mistaken! I'll see you later."

Undeterred, Evander delivers a solemn retort, "Go to hell Galgorn! That is, if a cyborg like you even gets that experience." His fervent hope is to never cross paths with Galgorn again. With determination in his eyes, Evander rushes back to the bridge, where Mal'Erro awaits with crucial news.

Mal'Erro waves at Evander, as he returns. "We're ready to go, I set the ships trajectory back through the wormhole and I managed to set the missile to launch, as soon as it emerges from the other side. I also set the ship to self-destruct just after the launch of the missile."

With a quick look at Angelica for affirmation, Evander authorizes Mal'Erro to execute the command. Moments later, they all hear a loud voice from the ship's intercoms, "T-minus 10 minutes to self destruct."

Evander and the rest of the crew look at Mal'Erro. Angelica quickly grabs hold of Mal'Erro and begins to run. "I thought you set it to self-destruct AFTER it got through the bloody wormhole."

Mal'Erro looks up at Angelica and replies, "I did. I calculated it would take 10 minutes for it to completely get through the wormhole after it turns."

Evander, in a state of panic, says, "Mal'Erro, it will take us almost as long to get to the damn ships! Then we must hope there's enough room in them for all of us!"

Mal'Erro realizes its error and starts apologizing. Racing against time, the group makes their way to the launching bay, scrambling to find ships large enough to accommodate their escape. With their vessels secured, they tear away from Galgorn's flagship, leaving behind the remnants of their harrowing ordeal.

As they soar away, a sense of relief washes over the crew. With the flagship hurtling into the wormhole, the plan unfolds almost flawlessly, as the missile, along with Galgorn's remains, hurtles toward the system's star. In a burst of fiery brilliance, the wormhole collapses, sealing off any hope of both Galgorn and his army's return.

As they fly toward Centima Four, with the base now in ruins, the entire crew on board watches the remaining enemy ships being taken care of. Evander figures it will be a good idea to inform the UPF fighter crafts not to attack their ship, as they are friendlies and not the enemy. While he is on communications with one of his fellow officers, he is informed of more good news. He puts it on speaker so everyone could hear. "It seems as soon as word got out that Galgorn's flagship was taken out, the pirate crew retreated. Also, thanks to that shimmer tip, we managed to get the upper hand by a small margin." The officer then ends the communication thanking everyone on board for what they did.

Amidst the quiet hum of their escape, Angelica turns to Evander, her curiosity piqued by the enigmatic nature of their recent foe. "So did he tell you why exactly he wanted you so badly?"

With a solemn shake of his head, Evander admits that Galgorn's motivations remain shrouded in mystery, offering only cryptic hints of his programmed directive for destruction and conquest. "He said something about a prophecy he read in some cave. I don't put too much stock in it, to tell you the truth. He also said something after I attached his head to the missile, that he will return. Don't know how. Could just be that he was too damaged to understand his predicament."

The revelation weighs heavily on the crew, prompting uneasy thoughts of the forces that may yet lurk in the vast expanse of space. Seeking solace in the possibility of newfound peace, Evander shifts the conversation, pondering the fate of the solar system that is on the other side of the wormhole.

Before Mal'Erro can offer insight, Blarek interjects, "The possibility of any other life in that system besides Galgorn or his army, is very slim. Look at what he was doing to other systems and how merciless he was at trying to annihilate everyone of us." Blarek gives everyone a grim reminder of Galgorn's ruthlessness, dispelling any illusions of mercy. With Galgorn's threat extinguished, albeit at a steep cost, Evander finds consolation in the knowledge that their galaxy is now free from his tyrannical grasp.

"So, what now?" Angelica asks Evander, with a gentle and soft tone. "You going to come back?"

Evander shakes his head, "Nah, I told a grumpy admiral that I would take the remainder of my mandatory time off. I think after this whole ordeal, that might actually do me some good."

Everyone is in shock upon hearing this. Kal'korg walks over to Evander, places his hand on his head, and declares, "Nope, no fever. Did you get another concussion?"

Evander looks at them all with bemusement. "What's with you lot? All I said was it would do me good, I still need to mentally recover and after this emotional rollercoaster we've just been on, I feel it's appropriate for me to take that time off."

Angelica comes over and gives Evander a hug. She then looks him straight in the eye, and says, "We're just shocked you actually opened up to us a bit more and not just bottled things up. I think time off has really done you some good."

Evander looks at her, and at everyone else, and just starts to laugh. This prompts everyone else to laugh as well.

EPILOGUE

Months have gone by since the tumultuous events with Galgorn, and a newfound tranquility blankets the galaxy. Evander is back to work, after a smooth recovery, more resilient than ever. Accolades of valor are bestowed upon him and his comrades, with a celebration in their honour. Admiral Sarklak is handing out medals to each crew member of the Olympus Starcruiser. When he gets to Evander, he says, "Just so you know, your parents would have been proud. You'll make a fine captain one day." Mal'Erro looks up at him, causing the admiral to question its motives, before handing the little robot its own medal.

Mal'Erro starts to roll around happily, carelessly knocking over the podium. Admiral Sarklak then looks at Evander, who gives a shrug and sighs, "I'll get it. I still got a few bugs to work out."

Admiral Sarklak shakes his head and turns to the audience. "Members of the Universal Peacekeeping Federation, I give you one of the finest crews of the…" Admiral Sarklak is violently interrupted as Mal'Erro knocks him flat on his back. In a daze Admiral Sarklak looks up at the concerned onlookers, and says somberly, "I'm going to dismantle that robot one day."

Meanwhile, on Centima Four and Prisalanti, peace has finally returned. Structures are being rebuilt and monuments rise, solemn testaments to the sacrifice of those who stood against Galgorn's tyranny.

Amidst the jubilant festivities that envelop the universe, a shadow lingers, unnoticed by most but felt keenly by one. Jalerg, isolated in his clandestine laboratory on a distant world, still on the run and hiding, toils ceaselessly, his mind consumed by enigmatic pursuits. He is interrupted by someone approaching, someone thought dead. He turns around and says cheerfully, "Hello sister!"

Kes, with a smirk, replies, "Hello brother, I see the first test was a success."

As they both laugh, they sense another presence enter the room, its form shrouded in darkness. With trepidation, both Jalerg and Kes turn toward the figure, their gaze met by a silhouette cast against the eerie glow of two piercing crimson eyes.

~~~~~~~~~~~~~~~

THE END ?

www.ingramcontent.com/pod-product-compliance
Lightning Source LLC
Chambersburg PA
CBHW070847250626
47159CB00003B/973